Redemption

Blue Moon Saloon
Book 3

by Anna Lowe

Twin Moon Press

Editing by Lisa A. Hollett

Covert art by Jacqueline Sweet

Contents

Other books in this series

Blue Moon Saloon

Perfection (a short story prequel)

Damnation (Book 1)

Temptation (Book 2)

Redemption (Book 3)

Salvation (Book 4)

Deception (Book 5)

Celebration (a holiday treat)

visit www.annalowebooks.com

Free Books

Get your free e-books now!

Sign up for my newsletter at *annalowebooks.com* to get three free books!

- *Desert Wolf*: Friend or Foe (Book 1.1 in the Twin Moon Ranch series)

- *Off the Charts* (the prequel to the Serendipity Adventure series)

- *Perfection* (the prequel to the Blue Moon Saloon series)

Chapter One

"Man, where are those two?" Soren looked around. "Everyone's ready but them."

Jessica stopped unwrapping the foil at the neck of the champagne bottle to chuckle. "I can guess where Janna and Cole are — in bed, snoozing or shagging."

Soren sighed. It was to be expected of freshly mated shifters in his growing clan. But really, could those two not drag themselves out of bed by eleven?

"I'll get them," he sighed and headed out the back door of the café then through the entrance of the neighboring saloon he ran with his brother. The stairs creaked under his step as did the wide wooden floorboards of the hallway upstairs, until he came to the happy couple's door and knocked.

"Janna! Cole!"

The giggle that had been drifting through the door broke off abruptly. Yep, those two were busy, all right.

Mates, his inner bear whispered sadly.

He let a few seconds tick by, swallowed away the lump in his throat, and knocked again.

"Janna!" he called, and even his inner bear winced at the way it came out. He hadn't meant to bark quite so sharply, though it sure did come out that way.

Happy, his bear reminded him. *Be happy for them.*

He was happy for them. Truly. It was just hard to forget that he'd once dreamed of mornings like that. Joyous mornings, waking up beside his own mate. Carefree mornings, watching her smile in her sleep. Sensual mornings, when an innocent touch or a quick kiss could so easily turn into more.

When he closed his eyes, he could see her. Sarah, his destined mate. His dreams had been full of her last night, even more than usual. Beautiful visions of Sarah tossing her hair over her shoulder and telling him about her day. Of her turning to look at him with those incredible emerald eyes.

What are you looking at? she'd tease him.

You, he'd say. *You.*

His perfect, destined mate. He could picture the sun shining off her fiery red hair and smell her huckleberry scent. Sometimes, it seemed so fresh and near, he could swear she was still alive. He'd woken that morning believing she might be walking down the street outside. She'd felt so painfully real, so torturously close.

He flexed his fingers, straightened them, and curled them again. A little ritual that kept the pain and anger at bay as well as keeping his bear claws tucked safely inside. Later on, he'd head to the woods and scrape those three-inch claws down the trunks of a few trees. He'd let his bear cry and roar everything he couldn't let out as a man. He'd rip at one tree after another until he was worn and bleeding and ready to pretend he was okay with the cards fate had dealt him for yet another day.

He cleared his throat and called out again. "Come on! Jess needs everyone downstairs, now."

It was an important day for Jessica: pre-opening day in her new business, the café right next to the saloon. In fact, it was an important day for each and every one of them — the handful of wolf and bear shifters who'd banded together in this high-altitude Arizona town. They were growing as a business and as a clan. Looking to the future. As alpha, it was his job to lead and coordinate it all.

Look to the future, his bear mumbled unenthusiastically. *Not to the past.*

Which would be easy to do if his mate were alive — and she would have been if he hadn't been away the night of the rogue attack she'd fallen victim to along with so many others who'd been burned alive.

"Get moving already," he said, as much to himself as to the happy couple behind the door.

2

He lumbered down the stairs and back into the café, where he snagged his second coffee of the day and thought of his grandfather, the legendary alpha, who had lived decades after his mate died. Decades that might have been his best as an alpha, because he lived entirely for the clan.

Soren snorted. Technically, that ought to mean he was all set to become the best fucking alpha of all time, because he'd lost his mate so young. He wasn't even forty, damn it. Not even close. He hadn't even had a chance to fully bond with the love of his life through a mating bite before she died. Hadn't had the chance to reveal to her who he truly was — or what he was. A bear shifter — a pretty damn ferocious one who would fight to the death for her, if only he had been given the chance.

He cursed fate for the thousandth time in the past year and shuffled slowly to join the shifters gathered in the front room to toast the opening of the café.

"They coming?" his brother — the only other bear shifter in their unusual little clan — asked.

He nodded and looked around. The other three present were all wolf shifters, two from neighboring Twin Moon pack and the other, his brother's mate, Jessica. The woman of the hour.

He took a deep breath and did as a good alpha should: locked away his own regrets and focused on the good of his clan.

"Okay, everybody. Here we go," Jessica said once Janna and Cole finally turned up. "To the Quarter Moon Café."

"To the Quarter Moon Café," everyone echoed with a hearty cheer.

"To a great manager." Tina, who'd helped them lease the property, raised her glass in Jessica's direction.

Soren raised his glass higher. Jess deserved it after all the work she'd put in at the saloon and now, the café.

"To lots more muffins," his brother added.

"To more working hours," Janna chimed in, wearing a wry smile.

Soren nodded to himself. That was the next problem he had to solve: finding more staff to run the saloon and the café. While their customers were mostly humans, it was safer to keep an all-shifter staff. Otherwise, it would be too easy for their shapeshifting abilities to come to light. That was the only thing shifters truly feared: exposure. Even though most shifters were peaceful, law-abiding types, there was no telling what kind of outcry would result if humans discovered there were shifters living among them.

"I found someone to help here all next week," Tina said. "After that... well, I'm working on it."

The shadow of a passerby drifted past the front windows, and Soren looked up in spite of himself. Damn those dreams he'd had last night. He was seeing Sarah everywhere now. Her flowing red hair. That smile that lit up his world. That tomboy spunk lying just under the surface of a tough, no-nonsense woman.

He turned away from the windows, shaking his head. He hadn't been raised to be a fool. He'd been raised to be the alpha of a bear clan, and damn it, that's what he'd do.

He forced himself to talk business with Tina's mate, Rick, the owner of a local ranch. That's where his mind ought to be — finding and pulling in new hires to keep the businesses growing.

But a commotion broke out by the front door, and he couldn't help but look up. Cole was leading someone in off the street, and the women in the café all flocked over to help. What was going on?

"Oh, you poor thing," Jessica said to the rail-thin woman Cole guided to a chair. Probably another tourist who'd had too much of the Arizona sun. So why did his pulse skip a couple of times, as if she were a long-lost friend?

"Rick, get her a cushion," Tina said.

"Get her a glass of water, too," Jess added, kneeling by the woman.

"I got it," Soren said, stepping to the counter for a glass. He counted to ten as he filled it. Damn, why was his hand shaking? And why was his heart suddenly revving in overdrive? It wasn't as if he'd witnessed a terrible accident. It was just some lady feeling faint. His inner bear, though, reacted like it was much more, pacing and growling inside his mind.

What? he wanted to yell. *What?*

He glanced outside as he carried the glass to the woman. Only a few weeks ago, a band of rogues had made their second attack on members of his clan. Were they back? Was that why his bear was suddenly on alert?

But there were no suspicious vehicles or strangers skulking about. Not much of anything happening outside on a Sunday morning. All the action was in the café.

He kneeled in front of the woman and held out the glass. The hand that reached for the glass was covered in wicked burn marks, and he winced a little, just seeing them.

"I'm fine," the woman said, straightening. The curtain of her hair parted, and Soren froze.

Everything froze. His heart ceased beating. Blood stopped pulsing through his veins. His lungs halted in midbreath, and even his bear went from rattling the bars of the mental cage he kept it locked behind to absolutely, positively still.

Her hair was darker. Her scent had changed a tiny bit, too. And she was thin — far, far too thin. But the second his eyes locked on those impossibly green eyes, he knew.

"Soren?" It was barely a whisper, but her voice shot straight to his heart.

"Sarah," he managed.

Mate! his inner bear roared. *Alive!*

It was Sarah. *His* Sarah. Alive!

He wanted to grab her and dance her around. To crush her to his chest and never, ever let go. He wanted to roar loud enough for folks all the way back in Montana to hear. To sit her down and start feeding her hearty meals to make up for whatever illness or hard times were responsible for making her so gaunt.

But before he could do any of those things, her hand dropped to her belly. A stretched-out, round-as-a-basketball belly so out of place on that thin frame. His breath caught as his mind slowly processed what that meant.

Pregnant. She was pregnant.

5

For a split second, his bear nearly jumped for joy. But then his mind caught up, doing the math. He hadn't seen Sarah in nearly a year — the time he'd been forced to leave home, plus the months since then, when he thought she was gone forever. Nearly a year, which meant...

The glass he was holding slipped out of his grip, and his vision blurred over red.

"Soren!" Jessica cried.

He barely heard, because his ears filled with a roar loud enough to drown her voice and the earsplitting sound of shattering glass. And his legs...

His legs wheeled and carried him out of the room before his bear leaped right out of his skin and mauled something or someone.

He couldn't think. Couldn't breathe. Couldn't react, not even to Sarah's beseeching eyes as they cried, *Please. Please, let me explain.*

Chapter Two

Sarah closed her eyes and slumped in the chair, ignoring the voices around her.

"Oh, you poor thing."

"Sweetie, it will be all right."

"Here, let me get you a new glass."

Someone swished a little broom and dustpan under her feet, clearing away the broken glass. All nice and neat. If only she could clean up the mess of her life the same way.

She was down to her last twenty dollars. She was so exhausted she could barely see straight. And the only man she'd ever loved — the only man she ever *would* love — had just turned his back and raced away in disgust.

Her mouth hung open as she held her head in her hands. She would have sobbed, but she was too tired, too shocked, too far gone. For a brief moment, her whole world had lit up with hope and light because some crazy chance had brought her face-to-face with the man she'd been dreaming of every minute, every day for the past year. Life had been so perfect when she and Soren had been together. It was only since he'd left Montana that everything had spiraled downhill. Fast.

God, how things had changed, and how quickly. Her dreams had once been filled with things like taming wild horses, scaling mountain peaks, or running with a pack of wolves. Adventurous, little-girl dreams she'd hung on to long into adulthood. But the past months had changed everything, and now all she wanted was to survive another day.

Or so she thought, because seeing Soren had suddenly made her want a thousand other things. The soft play of his fingers over hers. The scratch of his stubble on her cheek. The warmth

7

of his hug and the emotion in his clear blue eyes when they locked on hers. The solid bulk of him next to her body, so reassuringly close.

But hope was a dangerous thing. She'd learned that the hard way, again and again. Like when Soren had looked at her with awed, longing eyes, and she'd nearly reached out to touch his chin. To curl her fingers through his sandy brown hair, to brush her thumb across his lips.

A second later, her hope shattered like the glass he'd dropped — into a thousand tiny fragments with razor-sharp edges that glinted in the sunlight.

Soren hated her. Soren would never understand what had happened.

Her hands traced the swell of her belly, and she squeezed her eyelids even more tightly closed. No, no, no! She would not blame the baby, only herself. And while she might regret her own actions — God, how she did — she refused to regret the baby. No child deserved that. The baby deserved love and joy and happiness, and she'd provide that, no matter what it took.

But Jesus, she was one step away from sleeping in the street. The baby was coming soon, and she didn't even have the means to put a roof over its head or clothe or feed it or—

She caught herself rocking on the chair. Christ, these people would think she was nuts.

She wobbled to her feet and did her best to remember what pride was.

"Thanks, I'm fine now. I'll just be going..."

Which was nuts. Every nerve in her body told her this was the right place. She'd stepped off the bus into this dusty frontier town at dawn and walked the streets aimlessly, guided by the same crazy notion that it felt right. She'd passed the building four times already and kept coming right back, like there was a magnet in there, slowly drawing her in. Back to Soren.

Back to heartbreak, all over again.

She held her chin up and focused on the door. Whatever fate had decided to grant her dearest wish was a cruel one.

A pair of strong hands pushed her gently back down. "You need to rest. Rick, where's that pillow? Janna, get her a drink."

"I'm fine, really..."

She was anything but fine, and she knew it. God, where would she go? What would she do?

"Sarah," someone said.

She looked up and blinked at the brunette kneeling in front of her, studying her through stunning gray-blue eyes.

"I can't tell you how good it is to see you again," the woman said in a voice that cracked with emotion. "So good to see someone else who made it. Someone from home."

The way the woman spoke made it sound like she understood — really, truly understood the pain, the fear, the awful memories. Like she'd been through the same firestorm and came out the other side.

Sarah tilted her head at the woman. The face was vaguely familiar, but...

"I'm Jessica," the woman said. "Jessica Macks."

And just like that, it came back. The tall, gangly girl who'd been in sixth grade when Sarah was in eighth. The one her track coach kept trying to recruit but whose parents never let her join any teams or clubs.

"Jessica?"

The woman's eyes were moist, and she smoothed a hand along Sarah's arm.

A second later, they were hugging as fiercely as long-lost friends. They'd never been close, but suddenly, it didn't matter any more. Jessica was part of home. Jessica was part of her stolen past.

Sarah held on tight, and the first tears slipped out. "You made it, too?" she whispered.

Jessica nodded into her shoulder but didn't let go. "I made it, too."

Sarah's heart swelled in her chest. For months, she'd been haunted and alone. But finally, finally, here was another survivor of the awful night back in Montana. Until now, she'd only thought of everyone who'd been killed — like her parents and other good folks. Her mind danced with memories of the flames that had consumed her home and the inferno at the Voss place she'd seen on her frantic rush out of town.

But here was someone else who'd made it out alive. Sarah pulled back and looked at Jess through her own tears. She could see the same survivor's guilt reflected in the brunette's eyes. The same dark memories, though they'd been pushed toward the back. She looked around the café she'd stumbled into. Jessica had made a new life for herself, it seemed. A fresh start.

"God, it's so good to see you," Jessica murmured, wiping her eyes. She gestured to the woman beside her. "Remember my sister, Janna?"

Sarah's memories of Janna were vague, yet it still felt like a homecoming.

But a short minute later, the warm feeling in her gut grew chilly again. For months now, she'd been hunted by the same lunatics who had burned down her home — lunatics with an uncanny ability to track her no matter how well she tried covering her trail. She'd dyed her hair, lied about her name, and moved constantly — yet they always seemed hot on her heels.

Her eyes darted to the street. Would the murderers follow her here, too? Would they inflict their wrath on more innocent people?

She stood quickly — a little too quickly, because black spots danced through her vision and her head swam.

"I have to go," she mumbled, heading for the door.

"What? Wait!" Jessica protested.

"Wait!" several other voices cried.

She pushed the door open, making the bell ring merrily, and stepped into the scorching sunlight outside. Jesus, what had possessed her to get off the bus in Arizona, of all places? She'd been heading to LA, thinking she might lose herself in a crowd. There were all of three people on the sidewalk in this dusty town; it would take the lunatics no time to ask about a pregnant woman and track her down.

"Sarah!" Jessica called.

She strode on, pretending she didn't hear.

"Wait!" someone else cried.

She wished she could. She wished she dared, but her feet kept carrying her firmly down the street.

Chapter Three

Soren stormed through the kitchen, ignoring the protesting voices, then smacked the rear door open and rushed across the back lot of the saloon.

Let me explain, Sarah's eyes had pleaded with him.

But really, what was there to explain? It was all too clear how that baby bump got there.

Not by him, in other words. Not by him.

He stalked past the meat-smoking shed and the beer fridge, heading for the garage he'd turned into a woodshop. He would have liked to keep going and race straight for the hills, but he was alpha of this clan, and alphas didn't run away from anything.

Not regrets. Not their own stupidity. Not even their own failures.

And Jesus, did he have a long list of those.

He'd failed to make Sarah his mate when he'd had the chance, a long time ago. He'd failed to come clean with her about who he was and how much he wanted her. Worst of all, he'd failed to protect her the night of the rogue attack in Montana. He'd been miles away when it happened instead of at her side.

And yet, Sarah had survived — and thank God for that — but she'd been hurt. Burned. Scarred on the outside and probably inside, too, judging by the haunted look in her eyes. She was scarred forever, and he hadn't done anything to prevent that.

Jesus, maybe fate had spared Sarah just to rub in his failures even more.

Some stubborn part of his mind rejected the thought. Fate spared Sarah because she was good and kind and deserving. More deserving than him, that was for sure.

Maybe it's not punishment, his bear tried. *Maybe it's our second chance.*

Second fucking chance at what? Sarah was pregnant with some other guy's baby. There would be no second chance for him.

Redemption, his bear whispered. *To prove ourselves all over again.*

He barked out a bitter laugh and sank down in a dark corner of the shop. He buried his head in his hands and clawed at his scalp. Sure. He'd prove what an idiot he had been.

The rusty door screeched open, and a shaft of hot Arizona sunlight fell across his knees, searing him like a brand of shame.

"Soren," his brother murmured, standing silhouetted in the doorway.

He growled. The last thing he needed was a pep talk, least of all from his little brother.

"Leave," he barked.

But Simon didn't leave, damn it. He came in, one cautious step at a time, and then slid down the opposite wall. And just sat there, damn it, looking at him.

The shop was supposed to be Soren's refuge, his den. The place he could get away from everything. Any spare hour he didn't spend prowling the forest when work was finished, he spent in here, hammering away at the ghosts of his past. Chipping and sanding them into oblivion. So much and so often that he'd allowed himself to believe he'd had them all beat.

Until now.

"Close the door," he grunted. If his brother wasn't leaving, the least he could do was that.

Simon sighed and kicked the door, sending up a cloud of sawdust that hovered in the light. Even then, the door remained ajar, letting a crack of the unrelenting sun slice inside.

His brother let another unbearably silent minute tick by before trying again.

"Soren... Look, Sarah is alive."

His inner bear nodded eagerly. *Alive! Our mate is alive!*

Soren felt his eyes blaze with anger and a few stubborn tears. Of course, he was happy to see her alive. That was the important thing. But the shock of it all, the kick in the gut when he realized she was pregnant, and the bitter truth of his own failures — those stung. Deep.

"I gave up on her, Simon. I let myself believe she was dead." He kicked at the dust. Maybe that's what fate was up to: taking Sarah away because he didn't deserve her.

"We saw with our own eyes," Simon protested. "Her place was burned down, and the cops carried three body bags away. The only trail we could find was the scent of her heading into the fire, not out. How were you supposed to know?"

Soren closed his eyes, but that didn't clear his mind of the memory. Sarah's parents had run a trading post on the edge of the town closest to the forest they used to call home. The weathered wooden boards were charred black and still smoking when he'd gotten there two days after the massacre. It didn't take long for him and Simon to piece together what had happened. First, the rogues had ambushed the bear clan and killed everyone in cold blood. Then they'd taken out the neighboring wolf pack, and finally, the trading post.

"Blame the Blue Bloods, not yourself," Simon went on.

Soren nearly spat at the sound of the name. That band of extremist wolf rogues had risen out of nowhere with a hate-driven mission to preserve racial purity among shifters. Because they objected to the Black River bear clan mixing with the local wolf pack, they had annihilated both in an attack that came out of nowhere. And somehow, the Blue Bloods had learned about Soren's not-so-secret affair with a human and decided to eliminate her family, too.

If only he'd been there. If only he'd had his chance to fight.

"You think the Blue Bloods knew about you and Sarah?" Simon asked.

Soren let out a puff of air. He should have been more careful. The bear clan knew he'd been seeing Sarah, though they'd always tolerated it as a bit of fooling around by a hungry young male. It was only when he'd let the M word slip that the shit had hit the fan.

Mate? His grandfather had roared when Soren tried to explain about Sarah. *That human will never be your mate.*

The old man had even gone so far as to arrange for a mate for Soren without asking him. Without so much as *telling* him, in fact, until the day he'd announced it to the whole clan. And when Soren continued to see Sarah — because how could he stay away from the woman he was destined to love forever? — his grandfather had sent him and Simon away. Officially, it was supposed to be a time to learn from their East Coast relatives before coming home to assume more power, but Soren knew it was supposed to make him forget Sarah.

As if he could forget her. He'd sooner forget the feel of the sun on his skin in summer or the color of the aspens in fall. The majesty of a winter moon over snowy mountains, the sound and fresh taste of the creeks in the spring.

But it had all seemed so hopeless at the time that he'd given in to the intense pressure and told Sarah it was over when he was forced to leave home.

She'd seemed as gutted by the news as he was, but obviously, she'd gotten over him real fast. All her tears and insistence that she'd wait for him, all that talk about forever...

The image of the baby bump filled his mind, and bile rose in his throat.

He scratched furiously at his jeans. His grandfather must have been right about humans not knowing how to be faithful. Not the way bears did.

He'd dreamed of Sarah every day after he left Montana — and every night. Imagined a thousand different ways to make it work. He'd plotted and planned how he would stand up to his grandfather when he got home and how he would explain to Sarah. How he'd finally explain *everything* and finally, finally be able to claim his mate.

He snorted at how naïve he'd been. What did it matter how much time he spent dreaming about Sarah if she never dreamed about him? He kicked at the dust. So much for true love. So much for destiny.

Mate, his bear whimpered, filled with more sadness than anger. *All your fault.*

He hung his head. It was true. Some other guy had won Sarah over, and it was his own damn fault for giving her up.

"My fault as much as yours," Simon said, reading his mind.

"Sure," he growled. "Let me blame you. Let me blame everyone but myself."

His brother shot him a twisted smile. "You're good at that. Blaming yourself."

He didn't bother answering, because his brother had no clue what it was like to bear the pressure he'd been raised with. Soren was born to be the next alpha of their clan in the time-honored bear tradition of passing power from grandfather to grandson. He'd been raised to lead and to sacrifice for the common good. To live a caged life within a spider web of unwritten rules, expectations, and demands. Blaming himself was the one bit of self-determination he was allowed.

"The Blue Bloods, Soren. It all comes down to them." Simon's voice grew hard.

Soren let his bear claws out and dragged them across the floor. They dug furrows through the sawdust, then scraped against the cement beneath. Harder and harder, the way he'd like to rip at fate.

"One of these days, we'll finish what we started," Simon whispered. "Take out every last one."

Soren nodded. That had been their mistake — to stop after they'd tracked down and killed every Blue Blood rogue that had played a direct role in the massacre in Montana. It had taken months, and after that, they'd both been too empty to fight on. For every rogue they took out, it seemed two others joined what was becoming a widespread extremist movement.

Of course, there were good wolves, too. The wolves of Twin Moon Ranch who leased the saloon to Soren and his brother were gathering forces to go after the Blue Bloods themselves, but the wait was killing him.

"Take out every last one," he murmured.

Kill them. His bear channeled his anger in that direction. *Kill them.*

He considered. Maybe that was his best option — to throw himself into a counter-crusade. Maybe he could find redemption that way. He'd go down in history as the bear who wiped the Blue Bloods into oblivion.

He sat a little straighter. Maybe that was what he ought to do. It wasn't quite an idea yet, much less a plan, but it was the beginning of one. Sarah needed help; that much was clear. And because he loved her — God, he would never stop loving her — he'd help set her up for some kind of future with whatever asshole she'd chosen over him. He was honor-bound to let her stay until he got her set up somewhere else.

Her and the baby and some other guy? his bear protested.

The idea made him feel sick, but what choice did he have?

There is no other guy. His bear shook his head. *Didn't you see the look in her eyes?*

Well, he sure as hell had seen the baby bump, right?

Still, he plowed on with ideas he despised because his empty soul was desperate for something to strive for, even if it couldn't be her.

So first, he needed to get Sarah on her feet again. Needed to keep her safe from the Blue Bloods. Then he'd be ready to take on the rogues that had stolen everything from him — his family, his mate, his future.

And after, his bear rambled on, *we come home to our true love.*

He shook his head. The stupid beast didn't get it. There'd be no one to come home to, because Sarah had chosen someone else. If he were lucky, he'd die from his wounds, dreaming of his mate, a minute or two after the last rogue had drawn its last breath.

He frowned. If he weren't lucky, he'd survive, and life would go on as before. Empty. Listless. A wheel churning around and around, like his gut was doing right now.

He did his best to push that thought away. If nothing else, he might be able to live with himself. That was the best he could hope for.

Want a life with my mate, his bear sniffed. *Want her back.*

He closed his eyes and shook his head. Let the bear dream on. Inside, he'd be working on a plan. A plan that started with keeping Sarah safe.

Even with his eyes closed, he could feel his brother's suspicious look. "What are you thinking?"

"Nothing," he lied. "Nothing." He got to his feet, suddenly resolute.

"Now, why do I doubt that?" Simon shot after him as he strode out of the shed.

Chapter Four

Sarah didn't want to walk away from Jessica, but she sure couldn't stay. She hurried down the sidewalk, wondering what on earth she would do. Catch yet another bus? Curl up in a hidden corner somewhere and give up? Dig even deeper for reserves she knew she didn't have?

"Sarah," a voice called, stopping her in her tracks. It was deep as the night, as gritty as a mountain stream.

Soren.

She pulled up short. Wherever he had stomped off to, he was back and coming after her in a rush. His swift, sure steps powered up behind her, and the shadow thrown by his bulk sheltered her from the pulsing power of the sun.

"Sarah," he whispered.

She hung her head, wanting so, so badly to turn around and collapse into his arms. Big, thick arms that always made her feel so protected, so desired.

God, where was the capable woman she'd once been?

"I have to go," she mumbled.

The shadow covering her like a comforting quilt shook its head. "You just got here."

She tried remembering the vague plan she'd been working on during the long bus ride. "I need to go. I need to find a job."

"We have a job here." Soren spoke the way he always did, quietly and with authority. Leaving no room for a no. She'd have bet anything his blue eyes were doing that trick of theirs, too. Almost glowing with sincerity. Intensity. Power.

She slid a hand over her belly and gulped. She needed a job. Jesus, she needed it bad.

Her feet refused to move, but her head stubbornly shook left and right, saying no. "I need a place to stay."

"We have space," he insisted, coming up beside her. "Lots of space."

She didn't dare meet his eyes, but she followed the hand that pointed up at the windows over the café. Big, ornate windows leading to what looked like a spacious apartment.

Her heart skipped a beat just at the thought of a place to rest from running, if only for a little while. But how was that supposed to work? How could she possibly live and work around Soren?

You love him. He loves you, a little voice said.

She shook her head, remembering the hard look on his face when he'd stomped out of the café.

You need him, and he needs you, the voice went on.

Which was ridiculous. What did a man like Soren need from her? He'd probably moved on to a dozen other women since she'd seen him last. He'd clearly established some new business venture in this unlikely place. Whatever it was, he didn't need her. He just felt sorry for her.

He needs you like you need him, the voice insisted. That same ephemeral voice that had guided her here.

She stared into space, trying to still the thoughts spinning around her mind. She'd been so desperate for some chance — any chance! She'd be crazy to let it go.

For the baby, the little voice said.

She turned in spite of herself, and for one golden, sunstruck moment when her eyes met Soren's, she could feel love pulsing between them like it used to. A burning, eternal passion that would never, ever dim. It was like a physical thing, a lasso that bound them together and held them tight in its grasp.

Just when it looked like he might wrap her in the hug she so badly needed, his eyes dropped to her belly, and a cloud passed over his face. She nearly bolted then and there, imagining herself through his eyes. She'd let herself get knocked up by another man. And if he found out who it had been...

It would be best to tell him everything. They'd never had any secrets, the two of them. But when she opened her mouth, all that came out was a pathetic little choking sound. God, what had she become? She'd always been so confident, so sure. Even when Soren left, she'd managed to hold her head high for a while. But ever since the fire...

Her vision blurred, threatening a new onslaught of tears.

An arm brushed hers, and Sarah looked up to see Jessica, smiling kindly while she hooked an elbow around her arm. Her knees had been wobbling again, but Jessica's smile bolstered her.

"Let's talk, shall we?" Jessica said. "Girls only," she added, shooting Soren a look that said, *Leave this to me.*

Jessica led her back into the café, and Sarah didn't have the willpower to resist. There was something about finding a familiar face — one that didn't come with any emotional baggage — that did her in. That almost made her believe coming here hadn't been a cruel twist of fate but maybe — just maybe — a lucky break.

Jess shooed everyone out, closed the door, and handed her a glass of water. "Listen, Sarah—"

She started to mumble a protest, but Jessica cut her off. She pulled up a chair, and it scraped across the earth-toned tiles of the floor.

"Just listen to what I have to say."

Jessica took a deep breath, and Sarah did, too.

"You need help," Jess started.

She was right, and Sarah knew it. She did need help. Desperately. She needed a place to stay.

"I need to keep the baby safe," she whispered. She'd almost stopped caring about herself, but the baby... She couldn't give up. She just couldn't.

"This is a safe place," Jessica assured her.

"No place is safe from them," she croaked as the memories consumed her again.

"Believe me," Jessica said, "I know who's after you. They were after us, too — Janna and me. I didn't think we'd ever find a place to stop running. But we did, and it's here. It's a good place, Sarah. The Blue Moon Saloon gave us a fresh start."

"Blue Moon Saloon?" She looked up. She could have sworn the sign over the door said *Quarter Moon Café*.

Jessica jerked a thumb toward the wall on her right. "Soren and Simon run the bar next door. We started out there..." Her eyes went a little misty as every possible emotion passed over her face, from hopelessness to a flash of anger to a warm, happy glow. She sighed a little and looked around the café. "And everything worked out."

Sarah stared at the floor. How on earth would things ever work out for her?

"I didn't want to accept help, either," Jessica said. "But I had to. And you know what? Swallowing my pride was the best thing I've ever done."

Swallowing her pride. God, how often had she done that in the past couple of months?

But *this* was different than swallowing her pride. *This* would tear what was left of her aching heart into tiny bits, one piece at a time.

Jessica walked to the counter, poured two teas, then came back and set one in front of Sarah. She took a deep breath and started talking, starting all the way back in Montana.

"We didn't see the ambush coming." Jessica stared into the steam rising from her mug. Her voice was hushed. "They came out of nowhere, and suddenly, everything was on fire. Everything. The house, the woods, the neighbor's place..." She let out a long, slow breath. "And the voices..."

Sarah closed her eyes, remembering all too well. *Purity! Purity!* the lunatic arsonists had chanted as they burned her house down.

"I grabbed Janna and ran and ran..."

Sarah started rocking on the chair again. Yes, she had run, too. She'd had to give up on trying to get her parents out of the house and had run for her life, trying to ignore the burns on her arms.

"We fled to some relatives out East, thinking we'd escape the Blue Bloods there, but it wasn't long before we realized they had us in their sights again. Somehow, we could just feel it."

24

God, she knew the feeling all too well. That prickling warning at the nape of her neck, that panic building inside.

"We went from place to place for months until fate brought us here..."

Fate. Jessica said the word as if it were a living, breathing thing.

"Simon didn't want to hire us at first, and boy, did we have a rocky start." Jessica sped up, then slowed down, and her face glowed a little when she talked about Simon and the saloon and the new life she'd made.

"You'll be safe here," Jessica finished. "The baby will be safe here." She let a heavy pause punctuate the words.

A bird fluttered past the window, and the ceiling fan whirred quietly. An old truck rattled by outside. Sarah closed her eyes, trying so hard to resist the pull she felt deep, deep inside.

This is the place, the overhead fan seemed to whisper. *This is your home.*

Home. Did she really dare believe?

Jessica clapped once and smiled as if everything was decided. "So, lunch. Would you like a wrap or a sandwich?"

Sarah blinked at her. Was it really so easy to do what she had to do?

Jessica took one more look at her, then stepped behind the counter. "I'll make both."

Sarah plucked at her loose-fitting blouse and jeans. Did she really look that hungry? Probably. Just about the only thing holding up her pants was the baby bump, because she was rail thin. She shuddered to think what the stress of the past months might mean for the baby.

"No thinking," Jessica ordered her with a kind smile. "Just let go for a little while, and let someone take care of you for a change."

Sarah tried her best to smile. "Not sure I know what that's like."

"Well, you came to the right place. You want papaya or mango in your smoothie?"

She could practically feel her body crying for vitamins. "Um..."

"Got it." Jessica smiled. "Both." She gestured Sarah over to the counter and started throwing chunks of fruit into a blender — richly colored, juicy chunks of papaya, orange, and strawberry Sarah could practically taste with her eyes.

It wasn't long before she was licking her fingers from the best chicken wrap she'd ever tasted, bar none, and downing her first smoothie in what felt like years. The second she drained the glass, Jessica snatched it away, refilled it, and thumped it back on the counter along with a grilled vegetable sandwich.

"Oh, my God. This is so good," Sarah mumbled between bites.

Jessica shot her a weary smile. "It better be. We're opening tomorrow."

Sarah looked around the café. The walls were sparkling white, and every chair was painted a different color, making a rainbow effect. Tiny wildflowers filled the vases placed on each table, and an oversize photo of a nearly full moon rising over a magnificent desert landscape hung on the wall. The place was cheery. Upbeat. Full of hope.

In other words, everything she'd given up on.

"Your café will do great."

"You'll do great," Jessica said with a wink.

Jess kept the food and drink coming as she laid out her master plan without letting Sarah get a word in edgewise. "You can stay in one of the spare rooms upstairs and work the register here in the café. I'm desperate for help, and it shouldn't be too hard on you." Jessica's eyes dropped to the baby bump, and she smiled. "It'll all work out. Trust me."

Sarah felt like she could trust Jessica with just about anything, except foreseeing the future. What about Soren? How would it ever work out?

"We'll figure it out," Jess said. "Don't worry."

Worry was about the only thing she had — in spades.

"But... but..."

"But, hush," Jessica said.

26

The food was delicious, and Jessica's company was so comforting that Sarah gave in at some point. She ate until she was too full to fit another bite, and then followed Jessica out the back entrance, into the place next door, and up an uneven flight of stairs.

The building had to be at least a century old, judging by the high ceilings and airy rooms, but the place sure needed a lot of work.

"This is the apartment. I know it doesn't look like much, but it's getting there. You can have this room," she said, pointing.

"Really, I can't impose this much," Sarah protested, though the words came more out of habit than from the heart.

Jessica just shook her head. "I can't pay back everyone who helped me, but I can pay forward. And believe me, I have a lot of catching up to do." She smiled kindly. "Now, get some sleep. Everything will seem easier after you sleep."

"I doubt I can sleep. . . "

"Then just rest a little." Jessica showed her to the second room on the right — one with big, arched windows looking on to the street. The room Soren had pointed to earlier.

Every nerve in her body twisted and turned. Did Soren live in this apartment, too?

"Just rest," Jessica murmured, spreading fresh sheets on the mattress on the floor.

Sarah leaned against the doorframe. She didn't believe for one second that she would ever find any rest or that she'd found some kind of miraculous solution to her predicament. But if nothing else, she'd found a place for a brief reprieve. She let her eyes slide shut. God, she was tired.

"Sorry we don't actually have a bed."

"This is fine," she said, straightening before Jess caught her sagging.

It was more than fine. It was perfect. As perfect as she could wish for. Cool, clean sheets. A nice, soft pillow, and a second, firmer one, just perfect for curling up against. A glass of water at the bedside, the soothing scent of lavender, and a quiet ceiling fan.

Ten seconds after she lay down, she drifted off to sleep, wondering how soon the nightmares would come.

Chapter Five

Soren stalked into the office at the back of the saloon, congratulating himself for keeping his shit together long enough to escape back here. He closed the door, flopped into the chair, and stared at the wall.

Sarah. Sarah Boone, back in his life. His bear was still shedding tears of joy at the thought. His human side, too, but the joy was tempered by mournful thoughts.

Sarah Boone was no longer his.

He stared at the stacks of paperwork on the desk, took a deep breath, and promised his bear a long walk in the woods later that night. Right now, he had to get to work as if it was any other day.

Which was ridiculous, because how could he do that on the day Sarah had come back from the dead? The day he ought to have gone from *existing* to *living*, if it hadn't been for fate kicking him in the balls at the same time as it granted his most fervent wish.

The door squeaked open, and he looked up with a scowl, ready to cut off another lecture from his brother.

But it wasn't his brother. It was Jessica's younger sister, Janna. She crossed her arms over her chest and glared at him.

"You really shouldn't have run out on Sarah like that."

He sighed and scraped a hand through his hair. That was the catch about leading a clan full of feisty she-wolves who liked to speak their minds. They could and they did, more frequently than he'd like. Especially Janna.

"Janna," he started.

She ignored him and plowed right on. "You could have been nice. I mean, really. The poor thing..."

29

"Janna," he growled.

"She was barely on two feet and—"

"Janna!" he barked, and she went from lecturing to giving him the evil eye.

Soren glared at the youngest of his denmates. The problem with Janna was that innocent little sister thing she had going. And that she was right. What had he been thinking, running out on Sarah like that?

"Not discussing this with you, Janna. Not now. Not ever. Got it?" Janna might be right, but he was alpha here, and that was that.

She heaved a frustrated sigh and glowered a little longer before opening her mouth — again.

"Just think how much she can help. Her parents used to run the trading post in Black River. Didn't she do the books for them?"

Soren kept his mouth shut. Yes, Sarah had helped her parents run the trading post. A modest, middle-of-nowhere place that scraped by on doing a little bit of everything because there weren't too many stores in their two-bit town. Yes, Sarah knew all about running a business. And yes, Sarah was supersmart. The only reason she hadn't gone off to some fancy college was money and her loyalty to her ailing parents.

Sure, Sarah could help the saloon and café. A lot, because they were expanding before they really had the man or woman power to do so. He looked at the mountain of paperwork on his desk, though his mind was already running away.

To the past. To Montana. To the trading post. He and Sarah had known each other as kids, when they'd snuck off to climb trees and play knights in the woods. Sometime in their teens, they made the transition to sneaking off to make out in the woods, and he'd known the whole time it was destiny. She was his destiny.

His first time had been with Sarah. His last time, too, because he'd never, ever been remotely interested in anyone else. By the time they hit twenty-five, they'd all but claimed the abandoned cabin halfway up Cooper's Hill as their own, spending every spare day and night there whenever work allowed.

They'd make a fire in the stone hearth, make love for hours on a mattress he'd hauled in, and talk about fixing the place up some day. They'd carried water from the creek, cooked over open flames, and headed out on long hikes she loved as much as he did. She loved all of it — his outdoorsy, capable Sarah.

She'd make a great bear, his inner beast murmured for probably the thousandth time in his life.

"Earth to Soren, hello."

He pulled his focus back to the present. Jesus, he could really kill Janna sometimes.

"Good-bye, Janna," he said, pushing the door shut with his foot.

"Fine," she called from behind the door. "Be a grouchy bear. I'm going to check if Sarah is all set up in her room."

He nearly groaned out loud. They had a couple of spare rooms in the sprawling maze of an apartment upstairs, but only one made sense to offer a guest. Janna and Cole had the suite of rooms around the back. Jess and Simon had set up a cozy nest for themselves in the section of the apartment that stretched over the café. Opposite the bathroom — the only working bathroom, a problem they really, really had to fix soon — was a big, pleasant room, but it was completely unfurnished. No curtains, no bed. Which left...

He winced. That left Simon's old room, right next to his. He'd die living that close to Sarah without being able to touch her. She'd be torturously near, yet so far. He would be able to sniff her heavenly scent, hear the siren call of her voice, see her every morning and every night — but he'd never, ever be able to touch his true love, his destined mate.

Why not? his bear protested. *We love her, and she loves us.*

He stared at the desk, seriously considering thumping his head there a few times. Maybe that would bring the stupid beast to its senses.

She loves someone else, idiot. She slept with someone else.

And Christ, he'd pretty much encouraged her to, hadn't he? When he left Montana, he told her he was breaking up with her because there was no way it would ever work, not with his clan dead set against it. So he'd said good-bye and even encouraged her to find another guy.

And judging by the baby belly, she'd done just that.

Maybe you shouldn't judge, the bear tried. *Maybe there's a good reason.*

He clenched his jaw so hard it clicked as he mulled that over. It was his own fucking fault. Clearly, Sarah was over him. So why couldn't he get over her?

His bear snorted. *She loves us. Wants us. Didn't you see the look in her eyes?*

Yes, damn it, he'd noticed the way she lit up when he'd stopped her on the sidewalk.

So why don't you let her explain?

He shook his head vehemently. No way did he need to hear how she'd screwed some other guy.

She loves us. We love her, his bear insisted. *True love—*

He cut the beast off right there. *What the hell do you understand about true love?*

His bear just snorted. *More than you.*

Did he have to spell it out for the beast? *She's pregnant — by some other guy!*

His bear just shrugged. *Doesn't make her less mine. Just let her explain—*

He banged a fist on the desk, making the phone rattle and a pen jump. What the hell could there be to explain?

Anger took over for a second, and his bear claws popped out, raking four parallel lines into the oak desk. The desk he'd spent hours restoring, right after he'd finished work on the carved bar, back when they'd first taken over the saloon.

Stupid bear.

Stupid man.

Stupid bear, he roared. *Let me think!*

The silence in his mind was bliss, though he suspected the bear was only giving him the headspace to find a way to get back together with Sarah, which he could never, ever do. She was a human, and besides, an alpha wasn't supposed to beg for a woman to take him back. An alpha had to keep his pride, no matter what misery that might entail.

He schooled his spinning mind into a colder, more calculating state. Fine. Sarah could take Simon's old room. He wouldn't let it bother him. She could work as easy a job as they could create for her and rest her ragged feet. If she worked in the café — and God knew Jessica needed the help — they'd keep opposite hours, with her busy in the mornings and him working late nights. Every spare minute he had, he'd spend ferreting out the Blue Bloods and finding some place for Sarah to go where he knew she would be safe.

Safe, his bear nodded solemnly. *Keep our mate and the baby safe.*

Just the thought of someone threatening the baby made his blood boil. He would never stop thinking of Sarah as his, no matter what. And by extension, that meant...

He stopped short, because whoa, it hit him for the first time.

The baby could be ours, too, his bear breathed, and damn if his gritty voice didn't rise in hope.

For a split second, Soren's soul galloped away with the idea. He loved Sarah, so he couldn't help but love her baby, too. And hell, wasn't that just what he'd been hoping they'd get around to before he'd been forced to leave Montana? Every time he and Sarah had come across a hiker with a baby backpack, he'd wondered what that would be like — a pair of tiny feet bouncing over his shoulders and a cooing voice narrating all the wonders of nature as they walked.

Of course, those visions always involved a baby he'd helped make, but hell, Sarah could make a batch of burned cupcakes and he'd love them, too.

If the baby is Sarah's, how could we not love it? his bear demanded.

And damn, did it take a hard swallow to fight those thoughts away.

It'll be perfect, his bear rambled on. *Sarah will be safe here. The baby will be safe. We'll keep them safe.*

For a moment, he nearly nodded along. But then it hit him. Sarah and her baby would never be truly safe here, even with him ready to defend them to the death. The Blue Bloods had their eye on the saloon, and inviting Sarah to stay could provoke the enemy into another attack.

God, the irony. There was no one better to keep her safe than him, but simply being near him would make Sarah a target.

The baby, a target? his bear growled, and the hair bristled on the back of his neck. *So we kill the Blue Bloods. Get rid of them all.*

He wanted that — God, how he dreamed of that — but how? Where? When? The Blue Bloods were nowhere, even if they seemed to be everywhere. Eliminating them was a game of patience — and caution, because the Blue Bloods fought dirty and mean. They could strike any time, any place. A week from now. A year. The only sure thing was that the enemy would strike as soon as they found out Sarah was here.

He took a deep breath and forced himself to face facts. Sarah could stay with his shifter clan for a short time, but then he'd have to let her go. She was human; he wasn't. It would never work. Not with her, not with the baby. Not with enemies that would hurt them for mixing with his kind.

For their own sakes, he had to let them go.

Chapter Six

Sarah woke slowly and did a double take at the bedside clock. Had she really slept fourteen hours straight?

Wow. It sure felt like it. Fourteen glorious hours, blissfully free of the usual nightmares. She'd slept clear through the previous day and the entire night and woke feeling better than she had in months. She stared at the ceiling for a while, listening to the sounds of a household quietly waking up. A shower tap rattled from somewhere down the hall. The scent of coffee wafted from downstairs, and footsteps padded outside the closed door.

She stretched under the sheets. God, when was the last time she'd grabbed more than a short nap? When was the last time she woke slowly instead of jolting to her senses, terrified at what she might find?

Someone had set fresh, neatly folded clothes on the chair by the bed along with a towel and a Post-it note signed with a smiley face and a big letter J.

Sarah reached for the note with trembling fingers and held it close. As a kid, she'd kept an old shoe box and filled it with precious finds like white feathers and pretty rocks and a robin's egg.

Your treasure chest, huh? her dad had said.

She bit her lip and slid a hand over her belly. The treasure chest was gone, along with her parents, her home, and whatever innocence she'd managed to hang on to as an adult. But damn, if she still had the box, that note would have fit right in.

She took a deep breath and forced herself up. She was thirty now, hardly a kid. And she had a job to do. After

35

listening nervously at the door for a second, she stepped out into the hall.

"Morning!" Janna, the younger sister, called so casually, you'd have thought they had been sharing an apartment for years. Janna had one towel wrapped around her hair and another around her torso as she bounced down the hall. "Bathroom's all yours."

Sarah stepped into the still-steamy bathroom as Jessica called up the stairs. "Are you coming, Janna? Today's the big day!"

It took Sarah a second to register what that meant. Of course — opening day for the café. Her chance to pay back a little of the kindness Jess had shown her. So instead of soaking in the old claw-foot tub, she sped through a shower, combed the tangles out of her long hair, and hurried downstairs.

Well, she tried to hurry, but she ran into something big and solid as she turned the corner to the stairs and stood blinking for a second in surprise.

"Sorry," Soren rumbled. He'd been coming the other way, and now he was holding her by both arms while she recovered her balance.

Fiery tingles ran up her arms, divided into little lightning bolts, and short-circuited every nerve in her body.

His eyes sparkled as she leaned in out of habit — or instinct or sheer stupidity. A good thing she hit the brakes before she got up on the balls of her feet and planted a good-morning kiss on his lips.

Not the good old days any more, Sarah, she reminded herself, rocking back.

Soren's jaw hardened. A muscle in his cheek twitched, and she could swear he was reminding himself of the same thing.

She closed her eyes for a minute, fighting a losing battle to sweet memories of mornings not too different than this. Summer mornings when she woke slowly in his arms, feeling warm and secure. Memories of Soren nuzzling her, all along one side of her neck and face, then all the way down the other. Of weaving her fingers in and out of his huge, callused hands. Of

Soren looking at her with the kind of wonder usually reserved for the most stunning sunrises and sunsets.

She gulped away the lump in her throat and forced her chin up. "Sorry."

He smelled of pine and fresh air, like he'd been out all night. And if she felt refreshed after a solid night's sleep, he had dark circles under his eyes and a haggard expression on his face. An expression that asked, *Why did I ever let you go?*

She stared at him. His face held a trace of anger and bitterness, too, but neither was aimed at her. For a split second, she wondered if something had forced him to let her go.

Soren nodded slowly and relaxed his firm grip, though his thumbs stroked her skin one more time before releasing her.

"No problem," he said, all low and husky now.

His eyes were as mournful as a basset hound's, and she was sure they followed her all the way down the steps. Three strides later, she made it out the back door and stood panting for a minute. Which was crazy — it wasn't as if she'd nearly been hit by a truck. All she'd done was touch Soren.

But for a brief instant within that touch, he'd been hers, and when they slipped apart, it was like losing him all over again. Just like that day almost a year ago when he'd told her it was over, right before he left Montana. Just like when he lit up all over upon seeing her the day before, only to storm out the second he'd noticed the baby bump.

She ran both hands over her stomach. Yes, it was over, all right.

A good thing Jessica pushed the adjoining back door to the café open, waved her in, and put her to work.

"You're our cashier. Okay?" Jessica speed-walked through a kitchen thick with the tempting scent of berries, cream, and vanilla. Racks and racks of muffins stood steaming on the counters, and a timer dinged.

"Wow. What time did you get up?" Sarah asked as Jessica led her to the front room.

"Four," Jessica said without a hint of complaint in her voice. If anything, she seemed elated. Excited. Ready for the big day, as Janna had said. "You should have heard Simon grumble about it."

Sarah let a smile slip out. Soren was exactly the same way.

"Not morning people, those bear—" Jessica stuttered then hurried on. "Those brothers." She patted the cushion on a tall stool by the register. "If you need a break, just let me know, and we'll cover for you."

Sarah nearly laughed. Sitting on a stool was a lot better than some of the jobs she'd worked in the past few months to scrape together a few dollars.

"I'll make sandwiches, Janna will work the tables, and Emma will help you at the counter."

"Emma?"

"Another wol—" Jessica coughed, then barked out the next word. "Woman. Another woman we know."

The bell over the front door chimed, and a young woman with a long, dark braid stepped in. "Hope I'm not late."

"Emma, meet Sarah. Sarah, meet Emma."

It was about as much of an introduction as they had time for, because Jessica flipped the *Closed* sign to *Welcome,* stuck a wedge under the front door to keep it propped open, and greeted the customers who'd been waiting outside by name.

"Mike! Pete! So sweet of you to come to the opening!"

"Wouldn't miss it for anything," one said.

"Kyle!" Jessica shook hands with the customer right behind them.

"Mike owns Mike's Hardware, three doors down," Janna whispered in Sarah's ear. "Pete's a carpenter who stops at Mike's every day, and Kyle's the hot cop with the spiky hair."

Mike was sweet and friendly. Pete sniffed his coffee and gave a hearty thumbs-up. And Kyle... Yep, the cop was hot, if not quite on par with Soren. But then again, no man ever was. Not a one.

Sarah's mind started wandering over to the biggest mistake of her life, but she dragged it away again. The baby wasn't a mistake, and she had work to do.

Luckily, there was enough work to pull her mind away from several lifetimes' worth of mistakes. Within seconds, she was ringing up coffees and muffins and sandwiches to go. It was a pleasant kind of rush in which the customers bantered with each other and with the staff. A lot like the store she'd been slowly taking over from her aging parents back home, in fact. Everyone knew everyone, and they all faced their daily routines with smiles instead of complaints.

It was nine-thirty before the steady stream of locals started to peter out, which was just when the tourist crowd started to trickle in, spending twice as much money and time as the previous crowd.

"The saloon next door has delicious barbecued spare ribs," Janna said when they asked about other places in town. "You should try it for dinner. Twenty-five beers on tap, and a kids' menu, too!"

Janna was a born hustler, but she was more than that. She practically glowed with pride when she talked about the saloon, and her words came from the heart. She plugged Mike's Hardware, too, along with a few other places around town.

"Lazy Q stables has great trail rides..." Janna would tell tourists looking for something to do.

The stable, from what Sarah gathered, was just outside town, and Emma lived in an apartment above the barn. Sarah's mind ran over everyone she'd met, practicing their names. Emma had taken an apartment over from Cole when he moved in with Janna. Janna was Jessica's sister, and Jessica was Simon's girlfriend. It was like one big, happy family, and part of Sarah wished she belonged, too. Her hand slid to her belly, and she could barely hold back a wistful sigh.

"A tuna wrap and a soda to go, please."

She stuck on a smile and rang up the next customer. And the next, and the next, until at some point the door jingled and she looked up. It wasn't a customer coming in, but Jessica, flipping the sign back to *Closed* and turning around with a triumphant whoop.

"We did it!"

Sarah smiled the first genuine smile she had all day and tapped the side of the register. "A pretty successful day, I'd say."

The four women who'd worked their tails off all morning — Jessica, Sarah, Janna, and Emma — traded high fives, toasted each other with smoothies, and sat back for the first time in hours, enjoying the cool whir of the ceiling fan.

"We did it," Jessica said again.

"You did it," Sarah pointed out.

Jessica shook her head. "I couldn't have done it without you three. We did it."

We. Sarah let the word burn itself into her memory as she looked around the café. It felt good to be part of a *we,* and for a brief time, her hopes soared. Maybe everything really would work out. Maybe she'd found a place to stay.

But then her gaze wandered to the wall separating the café from the saloon, where Soren was probably just getting ready to open for the afternoon, and her heart sank. How could she possibly stay?

Chapter Seven

Soren slid behind the wheel of his pickup and slammed the door so hard, it bounced back on its hinges. The birds roosting in the nearest tree fluttered away in panic. He slammed the door again, cranked the engine on, and took off down the street. Not too fast, not too slow, trying not to beep at every asshole on four wheels, though the streets seemed full of them this morning. They weren't responsible for the crap hand he'd been dealt, after all.

He pulled onto the highway and headed east, keeping the windows down so he could feel the endless, open space. His bear demanded that he sniff and not just look at the ridge of purple-hued mountains rising above the line of dusty hills to his left. He caught a hint of silverberry and a whiff of honeysuckle among pines that gradually gave way to scrubby pinyons as the highway dropped to lower altitude ranchlands. The wind whipped through the cab, pulling at his hair. A loose scrap of paper flapped wildly around behind the seat — a little like his heart had done when he'd bumped into Sarah on the stairs.

Sarah. Sarah Boone.

Mate, his bear sighed. *Mate.*

He shook his head at himself. How long would it take him to crawl out of that weird no-man's-land he was stuck in — somewhere between sheer joy and utter dejection?

His hands tightened around the steering wheel. A hell of a lot longer than the forty-five-minute drive to Twin Moon Ranch, that was for sure.

It was crazy, the way fate worked. Not long after Sarah had set his soul on fire with that brief touch on the stairs, he'd been called to a meeting with Ty Hawthorne, alpha of the local wolf pack that controlled a vast section of central Arizona. And thank God for that, because another five minutes of inhaling Sarah's huckleberry scent and he would have gone out of his mind. His bear was so sure she was his, who knew what the beast might have done?

She's ours. Our mate.

He stared at the open highway ahead. Typical Arizona — long and empty and lonely, just like life without a mate would be. He ducked to look at the sky, wishing it were nighttime so he could see the stars. The constellations always made him feel as if he still had a group of clan elders to go to for advice. Not that they ever said much, but they'd be there. The Great Bear, representing all the generations past. Orion, the hunter, giving him strength. Sirius, the dog, sniffing out the way.

Scorpio, the poison-bearer, lurking, waiting for his chance to bite.

Soren had studied the sky every night he'd been out on the East Coast, where the stars were all hung a little bit differently, and he had tried to figure out a way to make things work with Sarah. Sometimes, he'd look up and dream of her. He'd dreamed a little too much, like when he pictured holding her. Kissing her. Touching her. It had seemed so unbelievably real, as if he'd wished himself right back home.

He snapped his attention back to the empty road and shook his head. No stars. Just the blazing Arizona sun and a pale blue sky that didn't seem to have a beginning or an end.

He clenched his teeth and remembered his resolution. Sarah might or might not love him, but he'd never stopped loving her, so he'd do everything he could to make sure she was okay. Her and her baby.

Some other guy's baby. He ran a hand through his hair and tried not to wonder who it might be.

He made the turn where the road intersected the interstate, drove a few miles north, then slowed to follow an unmarked dirt road west. Four bumpy miles later, he crossed a bridge over a dry creekbed, cruised under the gateway hung with the ranch brand — two overlapping circles, the symbol of Twin Moon Ranch — and parked in the shade of a majestic cottonwood.

He slid out of the truck and tipped his head back, sniffing deeply. There was something inherently calming about Twin Moon Ranch. Something peaceful, even if the troubles of the world were never really far away.

A door rasped open, and he turned toward the sound. Ty Hawthorne nodded as he emerged onto the porch of the slope-roofed building they called the council house. The wolf pack alpha even went so far as to descend the first of the three steps of the porch to shake Soren's hand.

Now that was something. The reigning alpha didn't come down to ground level for anyone but the most esteemed guests. It was a hierarchy thing, and wolves, like all shifters, were big on hierarchy. The first time Soren had come to the ranch, Ty had just watched and waited cooly from the porch.

"Hello," Ty grunted, gripping his hand hard.

Soren tightened his fingers in automatic response and tried not to let his inner bear turn a simple handshake into a wrestling match.

"Hi," he murmured, looking Ty straight in the eyes. No easy task, given the man's laser gaze, but then again, the wolf wasn't the only powerful alpha in town. He might own more property and rule a bigger pack than Soren — a much, much bigger pack — but Soren was starting from scratch, while Ty had the luxury of building on a strong foundation.

They kept right on shaking hands, harder and harder, and stubborn stares might have turned into glares if it hadn't been for the woman who appeared at the council house door.

"Ahem."

Ty Hawthorne — big, bad Ty Hawthorne — whipped around as quickly as a kid caught with grass stains on his Sunday pants and dropped his eyes.

"Hi, Soren," the woman said brightly, motioning them in.

"Hi, Lana." He nodded, hiding a smile. Leave it to the alpha wolf's mate to keep him in check.

Lana smoothed a hand over Ty's arm, and the tension in the air dropped slightly in response.

Soren took a deep breath instead of letting out his bear's sad sigh. *Our mate used to do that for us.*

43

He let out a slow lungful of air. Yes, that was the way it used to be. One look, one touch from Sarah was all it had taken to settle his soul. They said the more powerful the alpha, the harder it was to find a mate, so he'd always counted himself lucky, finding Sarah so early on. Little had he known that fate had been planning to take her away.

"How did the café opening go?" Lana asked as another car pulled in. Ty's sister Tina and her mate, Rick, stepped out.

"Um..." Soren started.

"Interesting," Tina murmured, coming up the porch stairs.

Soren tried not to grimace. *Interesting* was one word for it, he supposed.

When they had all filed inside, Ty led them over to a table covered in maps and got straight to business, much to Soren's relief. That was something he and Ty had in common — chitchat was not high on his list.

"We got word of another Blue Blood attack. Happened last night," Ty said.

The room went deathly quiet, and the hairs on the nape of Soren's neck rose. Blue Bloods. He could kill each and every one.

"They attacked a cougar-wolf pair this time," Lana said sadly.

Soren's teeth ached where they threatened to pop out of his gums. The Blue Bloods not only preached racial purity for shifters — they reinforced the message through vigilante attacks on any shifters who dared mix with other species.

"Not far outside Yuma." Ty pointed to the southwest corner of the Arizona map.

"Which might mean they're moving west," Lana said.

"They'll never move far enough," Soren growled.

"Either way, that's no solution," Tina said. "They'll just go on to terrorize someone else."

Soren met Ty's gaze again, and this time, they nodded in agreement.

Kill the fuckers, Ty's eyes blazed.

Kill every last one, Soren agreed.

44

The Blue Bloods had attacked Soren's clanmates twice in recent months — and since the saloon lay within Twin Moon property, those attacks affected the wolf pack, too. Ty Hawthorne was pure wolf, as was his mate, but Tina's partner was a human turned wolf, as were several other members of the pack. There was even a boar shifter living among the wolves of Twin Moon Ranch, so an attack on any mixed pairings was an indirect attack on their way of life.

"Killing isn't the answer," Tina insisted.

"No," Rick agreed, "But it's not like they'll respond if we go ask nicely for them to cease and desist."

"The underlying problem," Lana said, "is pack structure. Or lack of structure, I suppose. The more old-fashioned packs there are out there, chasing out any young males who might threaten the alpha's reign, the more the Blue Bloods find fresh recruits ready to fight for their cause. For any cause, really."

Much as Soren preferred the kill-them-all approach, Lana was right. Too many wolf packs — and even some bear clans — were ruled by alphas with iron fists. Twin Moon pack taught its next generation to respect, not resent the alpha, and the leaders made every effort to ensure that young males grew into fulfilling roles that contributed to the group. But that wasn't the case in every pack. More often than not, promising young males were chased away and forced to wander on their own.

Tina nodded. "The same kind of young wolves we've found to work honest jobs..."

Soren looked at the floor. When he and Simon had first wandered into Arizona, they hadn't been much different from rogues. But Tina had set them up with the Blue Moon Saloon and gotten them back on their feet. They owed her everything.

"...but rogue bands like the Blue Bloods seem to recruit them faster," Tina sighed.

He drew a foot across the worn floorboards. At least there'd been no danger of him and Simon wandering down that path.

"That's the thing — getting these guys before they're too far gone," Rick added.

Soren looked at Rick, owner of the ranch that bordered on Twin Moon property. He and Rick shared the same chronic problem — finding enough shifters to run their businesses properly. Hiring humans brought too many problems.

And shit, Soren had hired a human just that morning. Sarah.

Sarah's different, his bear said. *Sarah is special.*

Of course, Sarah was special. She'd always felt half shifter to him, with her love of the outdoors. And she'd always had a thing for bears that went beyond little-girl, teddy-bear stuff. They'd run across bears lots of times in their wanderings together, and there hadn't been a single time Sarah looked scared. On the contrary, the sight of bears seemed to fill her with wonder every time.

So why hadn't he ever told her who he truly was? Why hadn't he mated with her years ago?

"We're doubling the number of guys we send over to keep an eye on things in town," Ty said, interrupting his thoughts.

Rick nodded his assent; Seymour Ranch was providing back up, too.

Soren wished the saloon and café didn't need their protection. But it sure didn't hurt to have a couple of Twin Moon wolves hanging around, just in case. Janna and Jess were tough, but another ambush could come any time. And Sarah — Jesus, with Sarah around, the stakes got that much higher.

"What we have to do," Lana said, "is change the way some packs think."

Ty snorted. "That's like asking my father to change."

"He has changed," Tina insisted. "Well, a little bit."

Ty held his fingers a millimeter apart. "About that much, and that's taken years. Some old coots will never change."

"Victor Whyte will never change," Soren said, and the room went still.

"Victor fucking Whyte," Ty muttered, finally breaking the silence.

"Him, you can kill," Lana said.

Even Tina pinched her lips together and didn't protest.

Kill, kill, kill, Soren's bear growled. Victor Whyte had ordered the massacre of his entire bear clan in a cowardly ambush. Victor Whyte had had the entire Black River wolf pack wiped out in Montana. Victor Whyte had ordered his men to trap Sarah and her parents inside their house and burn them alive.

Victor Whyte wanted to kill Sarah and the baby, his bear grunted.

Victor Whyte, he was definitely going to kill.

He and Simon had talked it over a hundred times — going after Whyte before the extremist could claim any more innocent victims. But with the saloon just finding its feet and Jess and Janna joining them, they'd kept deciding to wait for the right time. Rushing off in a rage would leave their fledgling clan open to ambush, so they needed to plan carefully.

"You said you'd be gathering intel," Soren said to Ty, trying hard not to bark the words. Ty was alpha here, and he'd already done plenty for Soren's growing clan.

Ty glared at him then redirected the anger in his eyes to the map. "We have. We've tracked the Blue Bloods to a home base near Hope, Utah."

"Hope?" Tina shook her head. "They have the nerve to settle near a place called Hope?"

Soren thought of a thousand ways he could rip, tear, and pummel that kind of *hope* right out of existence.

"But if we go in there on a mission to kill the Blue Bloods, we're no better than them," Tina pointed out.

Soren fought the urge to volunteer to be the bad guy, just this once.

Ty dragged his nails across the map, showing the same kind of frustration Soren felt. How to do the right thing without stooping to the level of his foe?

"Which is why we're waiting," Ty grumbled. "We've got our own contacts, believe me. The second Whyte and his leadership team stick out their necks, we'll be on them."

"And until then?" Soren demanded.

Ty locked eyes with him. "We protect what's ours, and we wait."

Ours, his bear growled, having no problem conjuring up an image of whom that might be.

47

Chapter Eight

Contrary to Sarah's fears, the next couple of days passed quickly. Easily, in fact, except maybe the few times she bumped into Soren on the way to the bathroom or on the stairs.

But boy, did those moments stand still.

Her heart would pound in her chest, the blood rush through her veins, and her breath catch in her throat. She and Soren would both freeze for a minute, staring into each other's eyes, and it was like they'd vaulted right into the past, when everything had been promising and golden and good. Her whole body would warm up with hope and love and the energy that seemed to pulse between them like an electric field. Like magic. Like true love. Like... like destiny.

Then Soren — it was always Soren who snapped out of it first — would blink and lean away. His eyes would grow distant and cold, and it would be over.

Until the next time it happened, and the next, and the time after that. Little blink-of-the-eye moments she'd started to live for between the rest of the hours that seemed to drag by.

Not that she didn't like the cashier's job at the café or the women she worked with. It was just that everything paled in comparison to those fleeting moments of love and light and hope.

"Wow," Jessica said one morning. "Can you believe the café has already been open for a week?"

Sarah mulled that one over for a while, because it meant she'd been there for a week, too. Then another couple of days passed, making it two weeks, and she realized how much of a routine she'd fallen into. Work in the mornings, naps in the afternoons, followed by an hour or two at a desk in the back of the café doing the books, and finally, an early bedtime. And the next day, it would start all over again.

The routine became comfortingly familiar in its own way, as did her cosy bedroom and the comings and goings of her housemates. It was a funny little arrangement they had going, and a funny little gang. Two couples shared the apartment over the saloon with Soren — Jessica and Simon, plus Janna and Cole, with everyone spread out in their own subsection of the place. Everyone but Cole worked in the café or the saloon, but the close quarters seemed to work harmoniously. Of course, the two couples were both head over heels in love. Soren was the only single of the bunch.

Soren and her. And it seemed he went out of his way to avoid her as much as he could.

She tried switching all that off when she went to work, though her success rate... well, it was a little low.

Customers at the Quarter Moon Café were nice and cheery and kind enough not to stare too much at the burn scars on her hands. A crowd of regulars developed, and it started to feel a lot like home.

"Thanks, Sarah," Mike of Mike's Hardware would say on his way through every morning. She didn't even have to look at what he ordered to ring him up each day; it was always the same. Coffee with a splash of milk and one blueberry muffin.

"Have a nice day, Sarah," Pete the carpenter would flash his chip-toothed smile, put a dollar he probably couldn't afford in the tip jar, and head out with a chocolate-raspberry muffin and a couple of sandwiches to go.

The tip jar was Janna's idea, and it filled up every day, especially once she drew a little stork carrying a baby on the front.

"Looking good, Sarah," Jessica's friend Tina said one day, giving her a satisfied nod.

Sarah didn't know about looking good, but she sure felt better than when she'd first arrived at the Quarter Moon Café. Stronger. Surer. Rounder, too, because the baby seemed to be thriving with her new lifestyle.

"It's all the smoothies, wraps, and spare ribs I've been wolfing down," she said.

Tina stopped short, and for an instant, it seemed like half the people in the café froze. Jessica halted dead in her tracks as she carried another rack of muffins out from the back. Janna's head whipped around instead of taking a customer's order. The tongs Emma had been using to reach for a muffin clattered to the counter, and Sarah looked around.

What? What did she say?

A second later, everything was back to normal, and she spent the rest of the morning wondering if she'd imagined the whole thing.

Every once in a while, her old fears would catch up with her, and she'd peek nervously out to the street. She'd spent the past months on the run from an evil band that seemed intent on hunting her down. Would they find her here, too?

But fear became a passing thing instead of the constant, nagging companion it had once been. Jessica was right. This place had a safe, secure feeling to it. Jessica, Janna, and Emma were all tough, country girls who could hold their own, and it sure didn't hurt Sarah's peace of mind to have the burly Voss brothers nearby. There were always a couple of strapping young bucks from the local ranches hanging around the café or saloon, too. They'd settle in at a corner table by the window, eat enough for a platoon of marines, and shoot the breeze pretty much from the time the café opened to the time it closed.

The second a stranger walked into the place, though, they'd drop their happy-go-lucky veneer and stiffen like bodyguards on high alert. Sarah swore they'd sniff the air, too, as if their noses were keen enough to draw any conclusions from a person's scent. But a second later, they'd lapse back into lazy-cowboy mode, and again, she wondered if she'd imagined the whole thing.

On the other hand, there might be some truth in her bodyguard theory, because "the boys" — as Jessica called the gang of towering cowboys who rotated through regularly on their days off from work on the ranch — were always there. And

Jessica had instructed Sarah to charge half the usual price while serving them twice the usual amounts. It really did feel as though they were there to keep an eye on things.

"You sure you boys are all right?" Jessica would check in on the men periodically. "Not getting bored yet?"

"If you think this is a hardship, ma'am, you come try the food on the ranch. This here's a vacation for us," they insisted with their special brand of cowboy charm.

The boys read the paper. They played cards — until Jessica asked them to save it for the saloon. They told funny jokes with animals as characters, and bears always seemed to get the short end of the stick.

"How many bears does it take to screw in a lightbulb?" the one named Jake started.

"What did the bear say to the firefighter?"

"A bear and a hedgehog are walking in the woods, and one of them says..."

"Hey!" Sarah finally protested, calling across the café. "I like bears. How about you make cowboy jokes sometime?"

Everyone laughed then abruptly clammed up, and Sarah turned to find Soren glowering in the kitchen doorway, where he stood with a muffin halfway to his mouth.

Newspapers fluttered high as the cowboys suddenly found something very, very interesting to read — or hide behind.

The clock ticked loudly in the heavy silence that ensued, and when Soren looked at her and tilted his head, she swore she could read his thoughts.

Bears, huh?

The left side of his mouth curved up a tiny little bit, and she went warm all over to see the old Soren peek out for a brief instant. Serious on the outside but laughing on the inside. Happy. Smiling. Hers. It was another one of those golden moments when she could believe that somehow, everything would work out.

Yes, bears, she wanted to say. *You know I have a thing for bears.*

His eyes twinkled, and she smiled, slipping away on memories. They'd gone to the county fair together each year, and every year, Soren had looked on as she shot her way to a prize at the target booth. It was the only way all the rifle practice her dad had insisted she put in paid off.

Which one should I take? she'd asked Soren the first time she won, looking at the prizes. *The panda, the duck, or the bear?*

Soren had answered immediately. *The bear. Definitely the bear.*

It went the same way the second year, and the third, and she'd ended up with a collection of bears that crowded the lower part of the bunk bed her dad had built for her as a kid.

Soren stood in the doorway to the kitchen of the café, watching her with what seemed like bated breath. His eyes seemed to glow at her — a hallucination, probably, which either meant she was still crazy in love with him or about to faint from exhaustion.

Still crazy in love, she decided.

The corner of his mouth crooked a little higher, and she nearly sighed.

Then the bell over the door chimed as a new customer stepped in, and when she turned back to Soren, he was gone.

Sarah shook her head to clear all the crazy thoughts. Maybe pregnancy wasn't just messing with her body. Maybe it was messing with her mind, too.

Chapter Nine

Another few days passed, and just as the crazy rush of a Sunday morning in the café faded, business over in the saloon started booming.

"Gotta love the NFL," Janna sighed, heading over for her shift in the saloon.

"Installing those widescreen TVs in the bar was your idea," Jessica pointed out.

"Widescreen TVs, football, and Soren's special-recipe spare ribs. A deadly combination for the tiny bit of free time we have. We really, really need to get more help."

"You do," Sarah said. She nearly said, *We do,* but caught herself in the nick of time. She was just passing through. Sooner or later, she would have to hit the road.

But God, she sure liked the idea of leaving this safe haven *later.* Much later. Life was good here. She'd settled into a simple, honest routine that reminded her so much of home.

"You two are working too hard," she added. The Macks sisters had been working back-to-back shifts nearly every day at the café and the saloon.

"Until we find more help..." Jessica trailed off.

"And if we're ever going to get a second bathroom and renovate upstairs..." Janna added.

"Jess! Janna!" Simon's voice boomed from next door, and they both took off.

Sarah and Emma were still closing up when Jess popped her head in. "Uh, Emma? Can you help out in the saloon? Looks like the sports bar across town has a technical problem, and all the customers are rushing over here."

Sarah nodded toward her. "I'll close up," she offered.

"Are you sure?" Emma and Jessica asked at the same time.

"It's the least I can do."

They made her swear not to clean the floors, only to close out the register and do the books. By the time she finished, the saloon seemed busier than ever, so she went over for a look.

"Whoa," she murmured, standing just inside the swinging doors of the saloon, beside the faded old sign that said, *Check your guns at the door.*

The place was packed, and the football game was still in the first quarter. The poker tables in the middle of the saloon were crowded with extra chairs, and the booths lining the sides were packed, too. All she could see of the bar at the opposite side of the room was the top section — her favorite part — carved with a scene that might have come straight from home. A bear waded through a stream, a wolf howled at the moon, and an eagle soared over their heads. The whole bar was a masterpiece carved by some expert decades back — maybe as far back in time as the antique Winchester that hung high on the wall above the intricately carved shelves glittering with bottles of booze. The varnish gleamed with the light reflecting in the mirror centerpiece, and she suspected Soren, who loved woodworking, was responsible for that.

"Can you believe this?" Jessica bustled by with a tray of drinks, shaking her head.

Sarah spotted Janna and Emma hurrying through the crowd, too, delivering orders. Simon and Soren were both busy behind the bar, which Simon usually ran on his own. Even Cole was flipping burgers in the saloon kitchen, as she noticed when Jess rushed through the door. Everyone was helping.

Everyone but her.

Sarah bumped her way from the door to the bar, where Soren stood. His brow furrowed deeply as he juggled an over-flowing beer glass, a bill, and a customer's credit card.

She slid in behind the bar and plucked the credit card out of his hand. "I got this. You concentrate on the bar."

"But—"

"I got this," she said, tapping away at the register.

Simon pushed a spare barstool in her direction, and she took a seat to ring up the payments coming through. It was just like the café, except with bigger orders, higher bills.

That, and when the cash drawer slid open, something else slid, too. A couple of rolling cylinders clinked and clanked in a subdivided section of the drawer right above the dimes.

Sarah handed a customer his change, then picked up one of the cylinders.

A bullet. She held it up to the light and gaped. A silver bullet?

She peered up at the antique rifle hanging over the bar. A .44 Winchester, by the look of it. A furtive glance at the Voss brothers showed them both busy pouring drinks, so she jammed the bullet back in the drawer and slid the till shut. Out of sight, but not out of mind. Why on earth would the Voss brothers keep silver bullets around? A whole handful of them, not just a single lucky charm.

The next couple of customers paid with credit cards, but whenever anyone used cash, she snuck a peek at the bullets rattling in the back.

"Everything okay?" Jess asked the next time she swung by for drinks.

"Sure," Sarah replied, trying to get her mind back to work.

The noise in the bar ebbed and peaked. Simon's deep voice would call out occasionally beside her, while Soren stuck to nods and intense looks. Good old Soren, communicating more with his eyes than his mouth. He'd slam a glass on the bar, fill it with scarcely a splash, and slide it all the way down the varnished surface of the counter.

No wonder customers loved the place. There was even a pianist, hammering out a jaunty ragtime tune that could barely be heard above the crowd. Live music was another of Jessica's new ideas they were trying out for the first time. The football game was muted, and if Sarah looked away from the screen, the scene was as Wild West as she could imagine, right down to hand towels hung at intervals along the bar — the type used in olden days to wipe handlebar mustaches — plus a row of brass spittoons. Thank goodness the customers didn't actually use *those*, except for the occasional tip.

"Spare-rib special for table four," Jess hustled up to say.

"Pitcher of beer for table seven," Janna added a second later. "Can you bring it to them, guys? I have to get the food."

Simon looked blankly out over the saloon.

Sarah pointed. "Table seven — over there."

"You already know the table numbers?" he gaped.

"Sure." She counted them off. "Don't you?"

The brothers exchanged weary looks. Soren went back to pouring drinks while Simon went off to deliver the beer, murmuring something about women. Or had he said wolves?

"Another couple of hours like this, and we'll be able to afford that new bathroom," Janna noted the next time she swept by.

Another couple of hours did pass, and they flew because Soren was right beside Sarah, practically brushing her elbow. In spite of her weary feet, her aching back, and the ringing in her ears from the hubbub all around, it felt good. They didn't exchange a word — probably couldn't have, given the noise level — or look at each other. But that just made it easier. Each of them went about work quietly, but that was enough. Something deep inside her hummed with sheer pleasure, as if they were cuddling on the mattress in the old cabin they used to sneak off to and not standing behind a bar.

Yes, she was kidding herself again. Yes, she knew the feeling wouldn't last. But damn it, she'd take the little bits of goodness as they came and try to forget about the rest.

"Thanks, honey," a man said, signing his bill.

Soren glared — *Honey?* — and all but showed his teeth.

That was just like the good old days, too, when he couldn't stand seeing any other man come too close to her. So why, oh why, did he ever let her go? Why had he insisted on breaking up when he'd left Montana? Why did he tell her to find someone else? It didn't add up.

She glanced over at Soren exactly as he turned away. When he turned back, he was inscrutable as ever. Maybe even more than ever. The man wore emotional armor thicker than buffalo hide. There'd been a time when he let her in, but now...

She closed her eyes, feeling all the regrets well up.

"Tip is for you, sweetheart," a man at the bar said, and she snapped herself back to attention.

"Thanks."

Janna winked from behind the man's back. She'd brought the tip jar over from the café, and it was working its magic again. A born hustler, that Janna.

Sarah could sense Soren bristle every time a customer called her *honey* or *sweetie* or even *peaches* — which just about made her gag — but she put up with it because it was part of the job.

"Thank God we're in the fourth quarter," Jessica said, eyeing the TV screen.

They'd long since run out of spare ribs and desserts, but the crowd stayed on, drinking and cheering at the football game.

"Tip for the pretty lady," the next customer said as he staggered up to the bar.

"Thanks," she said in a flat voice while she made change.

"And for the baby," the guy added, waggling his eyebrows.

She counted to five slowly. God, she hated the gleam in people's eyes when they so obviously speculated about the act that created the baby rather than the child itself. As in, when and how and with whom.

Soren stood looming behind her — she could feel him there, with more than just body heat radiating off him — but the customer was too drunk to let up.

"That the lucky guy?" the man asked.

If Sarah could have wished herself to another part of the continent — or to a tiny cave where she could curl up and die, she would have.

Soren growled so deeply, she could feel it in her bones. She could picture the scene that was sure to unfold if she didn't do anything. The customer would make another stupid remark, and Soren would lose it. He'd grab the guy by the collar and jeans and pick him up straight off the ground. Chairs would scrape as people hurried out of Soren's way, and with a mighty heave, he'd launch the guy right out the door. Or worse, right through the window of the saloon.

Oh, God. He wouldn't. Would he?

A glance to her right showed her Soren's face, the scariest shade of red she'd ever seen.

Jesus, she could see it all now, right down to the hush that would fall over the bar as the glass shattered. The crowd in the saloon would gasp. The pianist would break off midnote, and the referee on the television screen would raise both arms in a mute call.

Touchdown!

She pictured Soren dusting his hands off and everyone backing up a step or two. Then Jessica — good old Jessica — would hurry the pianist into another tune and invite everyone to drink a discount round. It wouldn't take long for everyone to focus back on their drinks, but it wouldn't take long for the police to show up, either. Probably just as they were all kicking back and counting up the profits from the night.

"Well, that might have gotten us our new bathroom," Janna, ever the optimist, would say.

A cool breeze would whisper in around the jagged edges of glass hanging in the front windowpane.

"Minus the shower, maybe," Simon would add.

Then the toothy fragments of glass would flash red and blue as a police car pulled up outside, and when the cops asked Soren what he'd thrown out the window, he'd answer in a flat voice.

"Trash," she could imagine him grunting. *"Trash."*

A scenario she really didn't want to see unfold, so she pointed the customer to the exit. "Have a nice night."

"Bye, sweetheart."

She put a hand on Soren's arm and felt the tension coursing through him. Closing her eyes, she sent him calming thoughts, because Soren was Soren, and though he had a long fuse, she sure didn't want to see him get anywhere close to the limit.

She thought of the golden grove of aspens on the way up Cooper's Hill. The whispery sound of snow tumbling off pine boughs. The taste of honey, nibbled right off a chunk of honeycomb in summer. The soul-nourishing energy of sunlight pulsing over a south-facing meadow swaying with wildflowers. And slowly, surely, she felt the pent-up frustration bottled under Soren's skin ease.

The bar faded away — the crowd, the din, the malty smells — until it was only her touching him. Soren turned his forearm and slid it back until his fingers tangled with hers and played across her palm. For an instant — the briefest of instants — they were like one. The way she sometimes imagined it, when the boundaries between her and him melted until there was only *them.* A perfect, limitless unit of two.

"Uh, Sarah, you ready to ring up this bill?" Janna asked, cutting into her reverie.

As Sarah jerked back to reality, her hand slipped out of Soren's and went to her belly instead.

Soren's gaze followed, and for a moment, his armor slipped. His eyes locked on hers, so wistful yet so full of pain and longing that she could have cried.

I never cheated on you, she wanted to protest.

Except, of course, she had, in a roundabout way.

I never wanted anyone but you, she nearly cried out. But if she had, he could easily retort with something like, *Then why the hell are you pregnant?* And then what would she say?

His eyes asked her exactly that question as he took her in. Begged her, almost.

Did he really want to hear? Did he really want to know?

She wanted to take his hand — to stop everything, there and then — and hold it close. *Please,* she'd beg him. *Please let me explain.*

She'd wanted to do so ever since her first day but never quite got the words past her lips. Even now, she couldn't quite push them out. So she thought it, as hard as she could.

Please. Please let me explain.

Soren's eyes swirled at her, and for a moment, she thought he'd say, *Yes. Yes, please explain.*

But then a customer called for another drink, and Soren shook his head at her.

Not here. Not now.

And just like that, her chance was gone, if it ever existed at all.

"Um, Sarah. The bill?" Janna asked.

By the time she rang up the bill and turned back to Soren, his face was just as stony as it had been before, and another little fissure spread through her heart. She loved him so much, it hurt. Missed him so much, she could burst.

Drawing a weary hand over her eyes, she told herself to give him up and concentrate on the baby. That was her future. Her and the baby.

And emptiness, too? the little voice inside her cried.

An eternity later, the football game ended, and the crowd finally started to clear out. There was a rush of bills to ring up, but then a lull, and everyone who had been working the saloon stared blankly into space, catching their breath.

"Wow," Janna murmured. "What a crazy couple of hours."

Sarah stared through the warped pattern thrown by the water glass Soren had silently placed in her hand and nodded to herself.

No kidding. What a crazy couple of hours.

Chapter Ten

Soren wiped the last glass and put it in its place while Janna rinsed the sink.

"Holy crap," Simon sighed, flipping the last chair onto the last table that Jessica had just wiped down. "What a night."

What a night could apply to a dozen different things, but whichever Simon meant, Soren heartily agreed.

For him, that list of a dozen things could have started with Sarah, Sarah, and Sarah. Having her so close to him. Sensing her honeysuckle scent waft pure and clean above all the other smells in the bar. Hearing her voice and catching glimpses of her smile. Seeing the light shine off her hair. The natural red hue was peeking through the auburn dye, and seeing that made it seem even more like old times. They'd both been too busy working to feel the awkwardness that stood between them these days, and that felt good. Really good.

"Can I just say, we totally rocked?" Janna added. She gave Emma a high five and grinned at Cole, who was wringing out a mop.

"We make a good team," Cole agreed.

Soren nodded. They had been a good team. A great team, in fact. Their ragtag little troop of wolves and bears was carving a future out for itself in this unlikely corner of the world. Him, his brother, his clan mates, and Sarah.

God, she fit right in.

Her and the baby, his bear said.

He looked up, wondering if she was already asleep. Jessica hadn't allowed Sarah to help with cleanup, no matter how hard Sarah insisted, which was a good thing. Sarah was tough — supertough — but a seven-or-eight-months pregnant woman shouldn't pull as many hours as she had that day. There was no way in hell he'd let her help with clean up. It was a damn good thing Jessica had done the talking, because if he'd had to, he would have ruined everything.

He was no good at talking. No good at explaining. No good at saying all the things his bear had been trying to get him to say over the past couple of weeks.

Like, *Sarah, we need to talk.*

Or, *Sarah, I wish I'd done a hundred things differently.*

Or, *Sarah, I love you. Do you love me?*

His bear was so sure she loved him, and he was starting to wonder himself. She hadn't said a word about the father of the baby. Maybe the bastard had taken off? The way Sarah looked at him sometimes gutted his heart. Her eyes would fill with hope and wonder and regret — exactly the things that bottled up his throat every time he looked at her and tried to produce anything more than a choked sound.

But tonight had been a little more relaxed — if he could use *relaxed* to describe the hubbub in the saloon that night. A little more normal, almost. Well, *normal* was still nowhere near right, but better than before, anyway.

"I'm not sure if I ever want the sports bar's business again," Jessica said as she slumped against the wall.

Soren cleared his throat gruffly. He was alpha here; time to pep up his clan. "Good job, everyone. Thanks."

He locked the front door behind Cole and Jenna, who were driving Emma home. Then he waved a silent good-bye to old Harry, the cook, who left through the back door. Jessica's and Simon's footsteps dragged wearily up the stairs, and the saloon went silent for a while.

Soren took a last look around, turned off the lights, and headed to the office in the back, dreading the numbers he'd have to crunch at some point. He had money to put in the safe, tonight's receipts to drop off, and—

When he opened the door to the office, his thoughts broke off, and he growled. Not a growl of warning or anger, but a throatier, possessive sound. Sarah was there, sitting in his chair. She'd folded her arms, laid her head down in the nest of paperwork on his desk, and fallen asleep.

My office. My desk. My mate, his bear hummed.

He rubbed a shoulder against the doorframe, marking his turf the way he wished he could mark Sarah. He used to spend hours scrubbing his chin along her neck and cheeks until she went pink all over. Until she'd finally trap his head and guide his mouth to hers, and they'd get started all over again with deep kisses that were much more than just the prelude to another round of sex.

He watched her for a good minute, breathing the peaceful feeling deep into his soul. Not that he liked the fact that she'd gone right on working instead of going to bed — she'd started on the saloon accounts, from the look of it — or the fact that it couldn't be comfortable, sleeping like that. But still, something about the scene warmed his soul.

Sarah, in his place. Sarah, as part of his clan.

A dream come true, if only in a convoluted way. Still, he'd take what he could get these days.

The envelopes and papers spread around her were covered with sticky notes and pencil marks. Jesus, she'd already started color-coding stuff. He could just see the office a week down the line if he didn't stop her. There'd be stacking trays, calendars, and folders. Lots and lots of folders, all arranged in neat rows. Or worse, hanging files. Alphabetized. All that, and a chart printed in big, clear letters so his dyslexic brain could figure out what went where and why.

He smiled in spite of himself.

"Sarah." He tapped her on the arm.

Her shoulders rose and fell with every peaceful breath, and his heart raced from the warmth shooting through his hand where he made contact with her.

Mine! his bear sang. *My mate!*

"Sarah," he whispered, touching her hands. He rubbed the burn scars gently, aching inside. If only he'd been there that night. If only he'd never left Montana. If only...

He clenched his jaw and shoved the thoughts away. He'd beat himself up about that later, not ruin this precious moment with it.

"Sarah," he whispered.

Her fingers twitched, but she didn't wake up. So he slowly, gently rolled the desk chair back and lifted her gingerly in his arms. He cradled her good and close and spent a minute relishing the sensation of so much of her pressed against so much of him. She was too thin, but it was her. Still Sarah and still his, at least in his heart.

He sniffed her scent deeply, savoring it. Yes, it was a little different than he remembered, though he'd finally figured out why. She was pregnant, and that changed her scent. It changed everything.

Not everything, his bear murmured.

He held her a little closer and found himself nuzzling her gently. Almost humming with pleasure at being able to do that again. Maybe the bear was right.

Of course, I am.

Weary as he was, he wished the staircase was longer or that Sarah's room was farther down the hall so he could hold her for a little longer. But her room was right there, so he pushed the door open with one shoulder and knelt slowly by the mattress. The sheets were pushed back, so easing her into bed was easy. Letting go of her, though, was hard. Damn near impossible.

Just another second, his bear begged.

God, another second would be nice.

He finger-combed her hair behind her ear and settled down behind her, closing his eyes.

Just for a second, his bear promised. *Not long at all.*

God, what he would give to hold her longer. A night. A whole night. He wished he could hold her for the rest of his life, but even a second would do.

A second ticked by, then another, and he made excuses to linger every time.

Just making sure she's okay.

That was all he was doing. Checking that she was okay. And hell, it was nice and cozy there, and he was so tired. So, so tired.

So they lay there, spooned together, just like old times, and he had almost drifted off to sleep when something bumped him.

His eyes snapped open. The room was dark, but the street-lamps outside cast enough light to make out the contours of her back. The room was sparsely furnished, just like his, and nothing moved. Nothing but that funny little pulse under his hand. His hand was curled over her waist, his fingers wrapped around hers just north of her big belly and just south of her breasts. Neutral territory, so to speak

And there it was again, that bump. Not her heartbeat. More like a kick.

His eyes went wide as he realized what it was. The baby was moving inside Sarah. Kicking.

He froze, making sure his hand didn't sneak any closer. It wasn't his baby. He shouldn't touch or marvel or wonder. He really, really shouldn't.

But dang, the little guy kicked again, more insistently this time. Like it wanted to be touched. Maybe even needed to be comforted in some way. So Soren opened his hand and rested it on the curve of Sarah's belly. Resting it on the baby, in other words, and—

Holy crap.

The baby kicked, and he felt something between nausea and amazement.

He held his breath, wondering if the baby might do it again. Wondering why the baby kicked. Wondering if the baby felt his hand.

And bump! — another kick.

Strong little guy, his bear chuckled inside.

Alarm bells should have gone off all over, but all he felt was a warm and fuzzy haze.

Do it again, he wanted to tell the baby. *Do it again.*

Bump! went the baby in response.

It was ridiculous to think the baby sensed him, of course, but it still gave him a crazy shot of pride.

He's listening! His inner bear all but clapped his paws together in joy. *He likes me!*

Yeah, totally ridiculous, but it was past midnight and he was tired as hell. So if he was hallucinating a little, well, so what?

Bumpity-bump-bump, went the baby, drumming in two different places now. Was that an arm over there? A leg on this side?

Bump! Bump! The baby seemed to be warming up for a whole session of gymnastics. How did Sarah get any sleep?

He stroked her skin gently, trying to calm the baby down. Clearly, the kid was getting excited by something.

Mommy has to sleep. Soren sent the thought out as if it were his brother across the room and not a baby under his hand. Shifters could shoot their thoughts right into the minds of their clan mates, but most humans were deaf to that form of communication. Still, he did it anyway. Why not?

Mommy's been working really, really hard, and she needs you to be a good boy.

Why he'd figured the kid was a boy, he had no clue. But somehow, it just felt right. The way calling Sarah Mommy felt right. The way holding her felt right.

True love, his bear whispered. *That's why it feels so right.*

Soren chewed on that thought for a little while. Maybe the bear did understand the concept better than he did. Maybe true love was more about forgiveness than pride. Looking forward, not looking back.

He stroked a thumb over her skin, and his bear nodded.

Mine.

He didn't dare wonder if the bear meant more than Sarah by that.

The baby kicked as if in response.

Stubborn little thing, his bear smiled.

Soren took a deep breath. No need to get carried away on crazy thoughts when he was this exhausted, this confused. All that mattered was letting Sarah sleep.

Shh, he tried telling the baby. *Let Mommy rest.*

The baby went right on jumping like a little bean, so Soren tried humming. A really low, deep hum that was more vibration than sound, traveling through his chest and over to Sarah and the baby. He hummed a long, low note, took a deep breath, and did it all over again.

It took a while, but the bumping action calmed down and finally stopped. Which probably had more to do with the baby falling asleep than him humming, but still, it felt good. His dad used to hum to him like that at bedtime when he was a kid. Or maybe his mom? He couldn't tell any more, the memories were so dim. But it felt right. Like a bridge from the past extending into the future, in a way.

A really crazy, unreasonable way, because it wasn't his baby.

What if we make it ours? his bear tried.

A ridiculous suggestion, really. But he didn't care any more. He let himself imagine what that might be like. Actually holding a baby and not just touching it under its mother's skin. Seeing its eyes open, or better yet, watching it smile.

Getting to sleep was usually a matter of tossing and turning for an hour for him, but tonight. . . tonight was different. Peaceful. Serene. He counted the beats of Sarah's heart, hummed a little more, and before he knew it, he wasn't fighting a hundred invisible enemies but drifting gently away on a fluffy cloud of sleep.

Chapter Eleven

Sarah clutched at her sweet dreams the way a shipwrecked sailor might clutch a piece of wood. It seemed as if the storm surge of nightmares she'd endured over the past months were finally easing up and the sun was breaking through, because finally — finally! — here was a good dream.

Calm. Peaceful. Serene. She'd almost forgotten what that felt like.

She dreamed she was back in the cabin up in the hills, curled up with Soren. They'd gone up one winter weekend, a long time ago. Soren had built a big fire in the hearth, and they'd cuddled up under several blankets on the mattress. He'd spooned her good and close to his chest, strummed a thumb over her skin, and fallen asleep.

God, the things she used to dream of back then. Adventures. Passionate nights. Boundless horizons. But the past months had changed everything, and now this was her version of heaven. A peaceful morning in bed with nowhere to run to and no one to run from. None of the usual feet-mired-in-quicksand helpless dreams or the kind filled with silent screams nobody heard. Just a quiet, laze-around-in-bed kind of dream. Even the baby seemed to be snoozing peacefully away.

She sighed, stretched, and pulled the sheets closer. The cotton was so soft, it barely rustled. Then she went straight back to the dream and stroked Soren's fingers where they lay curled around hers. They were thick and callused and full of little nicks and scars, so she tugged his hand to her lips and kissed it.

Behind her, Soren stirred and kissed her shoulder, making her hum with pleasure.

Her nose twitched as a thought struck her. She ought to have felt his kiss on bare skin, but it was a kiss through a layer of clothing. A flawed dream, she supposed.

Then he kissed her again, and her eyes flew open.

Half the morning sunlight in Arizona seemed to be trying to slant through the arched window, and the thin curtain was barely fighting it back. The room was filled with a rosy glow. Birds were singing outside, and she was awake.

Awake, not dreaming.

Soren really was curled up along her back. Soren really had kissed her shoulder. Soren really was holding her hand in the perfect position above the baby bump.

She stiffened, and her heart raced off in triple time as she lay perfectly still. What should she do? What would she say?

Soren's thumb started to move over her fingers, gently sweeping back and forth, back and forth. He was awake, all right. So what to do?

She did nothing for a while, until, whoa — she realized that her fingers were stroking Soren's in return and that his chest expanded in a sigh. Those big hands clasped around hers, dwarfing them.

And the crazy thing was, it felt good. Calming. Right. Her soul sang, and her body did, too.

Which might have been why she eventually wiggled slowly around to face him. A stupid move, really, because facing him meant facing reality.

To her surprise, though, Soren's eyes were calm and blue as a summer sky, his expression somewhere between sad and wistful. Without saying anything, he reached over and rubbed a thumb across her lips. Over and back, over and back.

She almost said something, but what could she say? So she bit her lip instead and let tiny gestures do the talking. Her fingers stroked the fold of his ear, saying, *I miss you so much.* Her eyes welled up. *I want to explain.*

He smoothed his hand over her cheek, and that spoke volumes, too.

Then the baby shifted in a way that he had to feel, too, and she closed her eyes, waiting for him to recoil.

She waited a good, long minute, but Soren was still there. His body didn't stiffen with tension, and his eyes didn't blaze with jealousy. When his gaze dropped to her stomach, the corners of his mouth curled up a tiny little bit.

His face grew sad again when their eyes met, and his lips pursed as they did when he considered a problem.

A big problem, because even if it wasn't a brick wall standing between them any more, there was still an abyss.

She was the one who pulled away in the end, and he was the one watching her go.

"I have to go to the bathroom," she whispered, though what she really needed was a graceful exit. Some space to think.

She stared into the bathroom mirror for a long time before going back to the room where Soren lay right where she'd left him.

She stooped down to cup his cheek, and he leaned into her touch.

"Thanks," she whispered.

One word could never express all the emotions wrestling inside her, but anything else would have ruined the moment. She didn't have it in her to talk. And kissing or cuddling — much as her body yearned for it, she wasn't ready for more. She needed to quit while she was ahead. To hang on to the beauty of this morning exactly as it was. Nothing more and nothing less.

When she drew away, Soren sighed, but he didn't protest. Not even when she padded silently out the door and down the stairs. Maybe he needed to hang on to the dream a little longer, too.

No one was up yet, because it was Monday, and both the saloon and the café were closed. Not even Jessica, the only early bird among them. Sarah made herself a cup of tea, sat at Soren's desk, and sipped quietly for a while.

A delivery truck rolled down the back alley. A cat yowled, and a blue jay fluttered in the bird bath the neighbor had set up out back. Judging by the sounds filtering over from the street, the town was slowly waking up and getting to work.

So she did, too. Picking up where she left off, she leafed through the paperwork, organizing it into piles. A task just involved enough to keep the rest of her mind blissfully blank.

A half hour later, the stairs creaked, and a shadow filled the office doorway. She looked up to find Soren, wearing a pair of sweatpants and nothing else. Leaning against the doorframe, rubbing his shoulder against it like he had an insatiable itch, just like he used to do at that old cabin up on Cooper's Hill. He'd stand there and rub his shoulder and look at her like he wanted to rub her the same way, which, of course, he eventually would do once they got naked and—

"Sarah," he said. His voice padded into the room like a sleepy old cat. It was that quiet, that soft.

She was terrified he'd say something like, *We need to talk.* Something that would break this beautiful little make-believe world she was determined to hide in as long as she could.

"What are you doing?" he asked.

She looked over the desk, trying to formulate a nice way of saying, *Fixing this mess.*

She answered his question with a question. Safer that way. "Have you and Simon been keeping the books on your own here?"

Soren scratched his stomach at a point where one row of his chiseled six-pack abs met another, and she got sidetracked for a moment.

She shook her head and forced her eyes higher. "Um... Say again?"

"Just me," he grumbled, looking sullen.

Soren, huddled over numbers in this tiny space, she had a hard time picturing.

"Simon tends the bar," he said. "I smoke the ribs. Neither one of us is much good at bookkeeping, so we tossed a coin."

She could imagine her business-minded mother shrieking at that. *You did what?*

"What job did Simon get?"

It was good to have something to talk about other than the past. Something relatively safe.

74

Soren jerked his thumb toward the framed certificate on the wall. "Simon deals with city hall. Gets the licenses we need."

She bit her lip. Only the Voss brothers would run a business on the basis of a coin toss. But heck, it seemed to work. The brothers managed the bar, and Jessica and Janna handled customer relations. All in all, the business seemed to be on the path to success. But the books...

Looking back at the paperwork littering the desk, she held back a pained sigh. Soren had never been any good at numbers. She'd had to help him with math all through school. In fact, she was the one who'd taught him how to write his sevens the right way and not to flip around his threes. Soren was plenty smart, but he was a little dyslexic, and it showed in his ledgers.

Soren sighed, seeing her pained look. "Let me get some coffee."

She figured that was man-code for, *I'm out of here,* but three minutes later, Soren was back with a plate of muffins in one hand and two mugs clutched in the other. One coffee for him and a refill on tea for her.

She smelled the mug. Peppermint tea, just the way she liked it, with a spot of milk.

"Yesterday's muffins," he apologized, pulling up a chair. He opened up a ledger and grimaced at it.

Sarah watched him out of the corner of her eye. He'd grown up a lot in the past year. Hell, they both had. And though Soren had always been the quiet, serious type, she'd never seen him like this. So focused. So unhappy, yet so determined. So resolved to make the best of what he had.

He took a bite of muffin — which meant half the muffin disappeared — and ran his finger down the page. "I keep all the expenses here, and the income here..."

She blinked at the lined sheet filled with scratchy pencil marks. Even her technophobe father had finally given in and gotten a PC. Was Soren really keeping the books by hand?

"At the end of the week, I tally them here..."

She watched his thick finger run over thin lines of text, marveling at the self-discipline it took for a man like him to sit down and complete a chore like that. Soren belonged out in the woods. He belonged in a woodshed. A lumber mill, like the one his family had run. He didn't belong behind a desk.

He pulled out a slightly less worn notebook. "At the end of the month, I carry that over to here..."

She squinted at the crooked columns, the scrawly script. "This is your POS system, huh?"

He frowned. "PO-what?"

"Point of sa—" She clamped her mouth shut. "Never mind." Judging by his furrowed brow, he probably wasn't familiar with COGS percentages, either. She'd thought the bookkeeping system Jessica used in the café was a little basic until now. Poor Soren was using Stone-Age tools.

He looked so glum, she smoothed her hand over his. She didn't realize what she was doing until she'd touched down, and by then, it felt so nice, she couldn't stop.

"You did a great job restoring the bar," she said, trying to balance things out.

His downturned lips curved up a tiny little bit. "The bar, huh?"

Yeah, he knew she was trying to pep him up. He liked it, too.

"It's gorgeous."

"How'd you know that was me?"

She smiled. "I figured it had to be you, so I asked Simon. Three weeks, huh?"

According to Simon, Soren had spent two solid weeks sanding, removing paint, and filling in the dings before he'd put another long week into varnishing all those square feet of intricately carved wood and that smooth expanse of the bartop. Six layers of varnish, which meant sanding between layers, meticulous cleaning, a careful hand. No wonder the bar gleamed the way it did.

"Um...thereabouts." His eyes were bright with pride.

"It's amazing," she said.

He shrugged. "It came out okay."

"It came out great."

They sat there for another quiet minute or two, gently rubbing fingers, half holding their breath. Enough for her hopes

76

to rise that maybe the magic of the morning might last a little longer into the day.

But then Janna came bouncing down the stairs, and Sarah ruined everything by snatching her hand away from Soren's like she didn't want to be seen touching him.

Why the hell not? her soul screamed as Soren's shoulders drooped.

"Morning!" Janna waved, oblivious to the tension that had suddenly sliced back into the room.

"Morning," Sarah whispered, fighting tears that welled up out of nowhere.

God, she hated the emotional roller coaster of pregnancy. She hated tiptoeing around Soren when what she really wanted was to launch herself into his arms. She hated—

Her hand gripped the edge of the desk as she took in the mountains of unexplored paperwork. Bills, receipts, reminder notes. Soren must hate every minute he had to spend in that chair. Soren must have hated a lot of things he'd had to do to make a new start in life. If he could accept them, so could she.

"Listen," she said to Soren, trying to bridge the gap she could already feel opening up between them again. "Why don't you let me help you out in the office?"

"Don't need help," Soren muttered, getting to his feet.

Janna popped her head back in the doorway. "Oh my God, does he need help."

"Janna," Soren warned.

"Seriously, you need help," Janna insisted.

Sarah could see the color rise in Soren's face, but Janna plowed right on. Somehow, she managed the tightwire act of pushing Soren without actually making him blow up.

"Hey, I know you do your best," Janna said. "But Sarah's a total pro. You should see how fast she does the books for the café." She rolled a wrist and snapped her fingers. "Like that. She's amazing."

Soren glared at Janna, but she didn't seem to notice. She just pointed at his chest and tapped once or twice. "Just think. Lots more time for you to spend in the woodshop."

Soren squeezed his lips, but Sarah caught the wistful glance he shot in that direction.

"Lots more time hiking or running or whatever it is you bear—" Janna coughed and sputtered on quickly. "Brothers! Whatever you brothers do out there in the woods."

Sarah followed Soren's gaze out the upper edge of the windowpane, where he'd be able to see the green blanket of the national forest that started not too far from town.

"I'm happy to help," Sarah said.

"You're doing enough." He shook his head.

"A couple of hours sitting in a chair working a cash register hardly seems like enough."

"Believe me, it's enough," he shot back. "Especially when you're...you're..." He waved his hand in the air, not quite able to produce the word.

Janna arched an eyebrow and filled in what neither of them was ready to say. "Pregnant?"

Soren opened his mouth, then closed it without saying anything. His eyes churned and filled with pain.

God, there it was again. The one thing standing between them. The abyss.

"Which reminds me," Janna said brightly, either ignoring or completely oblivious to the tension in the air. "Your appointment is at ten."

"Appointment?" Sarah and Soren asked at the same time.

"Sure. With the obstetrician. Remember? Jessica made it for you."

Sarah groaned. She'd been putting off a checkup, not ready to face those details of reality just yet, but Jessica had insisted.

"Oh!" Janna's face fell as she remembered something. "We need to find you a ride."

"A ride?"

"Jessica was going to take you, but the inspector is coming for a follow-up visit to the café today. Which reminds me, I need to get cleaning..." Janna trailed off. "Damn! That means I can't take you, either."

"No problem." Sarah flapped her hands quickly. "I'll take a cab." She'd do anything to end the subject now, before Soren looked any more pained.

"Don't be silly. Oh!" Janna announced. "Soren can take you."

Sarah froze. Soren drew back.

"Um. . ." they both mumbled at the same time.

"Why not?" Janna insisted. "You've got the day off, boss." She lifted an eyebrow at Soren.

"So does Simon," he tried.

"Ha," Janna said. "Do you really want him to take her to this appointment?"

Sarah worked up the nerve to drag her eyes from the carpet to Soren's face, which was twisted with a look that said, *Do you really want* me *to take her?*

But Janna insisted, and when Jess came down, she insisted, too.

"It's not like you need to go in, Soren. Just drive her, for goodness' sake."

The sisters goaded them through the next hour and right into the car at a quarter to ten.

"See you later!" Janna called cheerily.

"See you later," Jess waved.

"See you later," Sarah mumbled from the front seat, studying her feet as Soren pulled wordlessly out onto the street.

Chapter Twelve

Soren drove, thinking of all the different ways he'd kill Janna the next chance he got. He'd kill her, then Jessica, then move to some place in Alaska where he could shift permanently into bear form and never, ever have to deal with shit like this again.

Taking Sarah to a doctor's appointment for a baby that wasn't his?

His bear, however, was suddenly concerned. Deeply, deeply concerned. Biting-his-claws-nervously kind of concerned.

Doctor? Is something wrong with the baby?

There's nothing wrong with the baby, he growled back.

How can you be sure?

I'm sure, he snapped.

But what if? Babies need doctors, right? the bear fretted.

Mom didn't go to a doctor. Grandma didn't go to a doctor. Aunt Lucille didn't go to a doctor.

The bear paced in the mental cage Soren kept him locked inside. *But Sarah is human. Humans need doctors.*

She'll be fine! he growled back.

What about the baby?

The baby will be fine, too, damn it!

"Did you say something?" Sarah, who'd been awfully quiet, asked.

He shook his head and hurled a curse at his bear, but the damage had been done. Now he was nervous, too. What if the baby wasn't okay? Sarah had been awfully thin when she'd first come to the saloon. That couldn't be good for a developing baby. What if there was something really important that had to be caught right now?

81

He drove a little faster. And damn it, a parking space opened up right in front of the doctor's office, so he didn't have an excuse not to walk her in. And — double damn it — he didn't have the heart to abandon Sarah in a waiting room full of strangers, either, so he ended up waiting with her, too. Eyeing the clock. Praying for salvation. Planning twenty different tortures he'd subject Victor Whyte and the Blue Blood leadership to when he finally got his chance, because they had set this whole mess into motion. They were the ones to blame. Jesus, he ought to be out hunting the enemy down, not sitting in an air-conditioned room praying for each stubborn second to pass.

Shit, shit, shit.

He looked out the window. Checked the laces of his boots. Stared at the ceiling then at the back of his hands. Jesus, how was he supposed to last five minutes there?

Somehow, he lasted fifteen and was about to make a hasty escape when an attendant came in and called Sarah's name. When she led Sarah to one room and him to another, he relaxed a little bit, figuring they'd have mercy and leave him in peace for a while.

But no. The door popped open a second later, and in came Sarah with a cup of urine and the same attendant as before. The woman ignored him completely, put the cup on a tray, and took Sarah's blood pressure and pulse.

"Um..." he tried, measuring the distance to the door with his eyes. He could go now, right? He wasn't the father. He wasn't exactly a friend. He was in that no-man's-land in between.

"The doctor will be here in a second," the lady said.

He didn't want the doctor. He wanted out.

But it was too late, because the doctor hustled in — an older lady with a scary upswept hairdo and a very white coat — and shook everyone's hand.

"Mrs. Boone? Mr. Boone? Hello."

Boone? Boone was Sarah's father, not him. He was a Voss, for Christ's sake!

But Sarah looked so lonely, so lost, that he couldn't help but clear his throat and whisper when the doctor turned away.

"Maybe I should go now."

For a split second, abject fear crossed her eyes — an emotion his tough, übercapable girl never, ever showed — until she blinked and hid it away.

"I'm fine. You can go," she said, straightening her shoulders in a move he knew was just for show.

"Um, I can stay if you want," he offered — really, really quietly, so that maybe she wouldn't hear.

"Um... That would be okay." The forced nonchalance in her voice couldn't cover up the note of hope. So, shit, his fate was sealed.

The doctor turned back to them and then the questions started, followed by the examination, and things got progressively worse, culminating in the moment when Sarah had to strip from the waist down and climb into an elevated chair surrounded by instruments of torture of some kind.

Soren made himself as small as possible — next to impossible for a bear — and tried really hard not to look, not to think, and preferably, not to exist. To clear his mind and think of anything, anything but this. Sarah naked and turned on was the most beautiful thing in the world. Sarah spread out in an examining room was... was... Well, it was just wrong.

"Now, let's go back to conception," the doctor said, snapping on a pair of gloves.

Sarah sucked in her lips. Soren ground his teeth.

"When do you estimate it would have been?" The doctor started spreading goop over Sarah's stomach.

When? Sometime when he'd been two thousand fucking miles away.

"October third," Sarah whispered in a sad voice full of infinite regrets.

His head snapped up.

Sarah looked him straight in the eye and nodded. "October third."

His birthday. His fucking birthday. He rolled his foot over a power cord lying on the tiled floor.

"Now, it's rare to know the exact date," the doctor commented with a smile.

"It was the only time," Sarah whispered. "The one time."

If that was supposed to make him feel better, it didn't. She'd slept with someone on his birthday? Great. The very night he'd been dreaming of her, she'd been with someone else.

God, the past couple of days had gone so smoothly, he'd started wondering if they might patch things up. But now...

The doctor looked at Sarah in surprise, then looked at him. "October third?"

See? He wanted to yell. *It wasn't me. It should have been, but it wasn't.*

"Well, well," the doctor murmured, clearly wondering what was wrong with their sex life. Then she pulled out a penis-shaped contraption from her toolbox and brandished it under his nose. "The better to see your baby with."

Not my baby, he wanted to growl. But it felt wrong to even think such a thing. The baby deserved better. The baby deserved to be loved.

I love the baby, his bear whispered inside.

"Let's have a closer look," the doctor said, turning on a screen.

Soren squeezed his eyes as tight as he could. Look? How could a guy be expected to look?

"So, there's the head..."

God, he was starting to feel sick.

"The kidneys are developing well..."

Kidneys? He blanched. He figured this would be a girl/boy, five fingers/five toes kind of thing, not an anatomy lesson.

"This is quite a big baby for thirty weeks," the doc went on. "Big hands, too."

Soren looked at his own hand, scowling. His mom had always said that about him. It seemed like her favorite thing, sharing too much information about him as a baby. She'd laugh and smile and go all misty-eyed and babble on about embarrassing baby things. *My big baby bear with his big bear hands,* his mom used to say.

Yeah, he used to grumble. She said that about Simon, too.

And wait a minute. Hadn't his aunt said the same thing about his cousins?

He sat a little straighter, trying to remember the last baby to be born to the clan. It had been a good long time ago. He'd been about twelve and couldn't have cared less. All he vaguely remembered was a group of excited women gathered around a cradle.

That's a good bear baby, one of the older women had said. *You can always tell a bear. Big body, big hands.*

"Oh, what's this?" the doctor said, sounding concerned.

Sarah looked up in alarm. "What's wrong?"

"Oh, nothing," the doctor said quickly. "It's just that I caught a glimpse of something..."

Soren glanced at the monitor. The doctor turned the probe around Sarah's private parts, panning the view. "Hmmm. Let me get my glasses..."

He clenched and unclenched his hands. Big baby, big hands...

Fuck. What if the father wasn't human? What if the father was a bear?

He looked at Sarah, who was studying the screen in concern. The image didn't resemble a human or a bear so much as an alien of some kind.

His mind spun. Surely Sarah hadn't slept with one of the guys from his clan? His cousin Todd had promised to keep Sarah safe while Soren was gone, and Todd had never said anything about Sarah showing any interest in another bear shifter. Not that Sarah would know the difference between a shifter and human, but still.

The doctor stuck a pair of glasses on her nose and turned to the screen.

Soren had no clue if the baby was a shifter or not, and he had no clue if shifter babies were recognizable in ultrasounds. But he sure as hell wasn't going to find out the hard way. He wrapped a foot around the power cord to the monitor and yanked it out of the socket.

"Oh!" the doctor cried, watching the screen go black.

"Oh?" Sarah looked at the doctor, more anxious than ever.

Soren kicked the cord out of sight as the doctor went around the room, flicking the lights on and off.

"We didn't seem to lose power," she murmured.

God, Soren hoped she was better with babies than she was with circuitry.

Two more women hustled in and started rooting around. And Jesus, there was poor Sarah, high and dry on that damn examining chair, worried and helpless and alone. He grabbed her hand and shoved her clothes at her.

"We're out of here."

"Soren!" she protested.

"We're out of here."

"But..."

"We have to go."

"But why?" Sarah pulled back.

He ground his teeth. "We have to talk."

"Talk?" she gaped at him. "You want to talk now?"

∞∞∞∞

He drove clear out of town and up into the hills, wondering desperately how he'd start the talk neither of them wanted to have. His inner autopilot led him to the state park he usually headed to when he needed to let his bear out, where he parked and led Sarah — tight-lipped, angry Sarah — out to the first of two lakes. The water was blue and calm, reflecting a gorgeous Arizona sky, the red rock outcrops, and the green of the pines on the surrounding hills. It was one of his favorite places — so calm and serene. Which didn't seem to help, though, because after pacing for a few minutes, he ended up blurting it out.

"Who's the father?"

Sarah closed her eyes and crossed her arms over her chest.

"Sarah, I need to know."

Her eyes flew open, and boy did she look mad. "Why would you *need* to know?"

God, he wished he could just speak the truth. *Because if that baby is a shifter, it changes everything.*

If the baby is a shifter, there's nothing stopping us from get-ting to keep you forever. Both of you, his bear added breath-lessly.

Soren kept his mouth shut and waited her out.

A bird sang in the bushes, and a light breeze whispered through the trees. A fish splashed at the surface of the lake, sending ripples in ever-widening circles across the wobbly re-flection of the sky. And for some strange reason, he thought of the baby, bumping his hand.

If that baby was a bear shifter, it was his to take care of as part of his clan.

If the baby was human, he would have to stick to the origi-nal plan of finding Sarah a place far away to live her life without him. It would be safer for her and the baby not to mix with shifters and draw the attention of the Blue Bloods.

I want it to be a shifter, his bear whispered inside.

I want it to be, too, he found himself agreeing.

But if it was? Crap, how would he ever explain?

"I'll tell... if you promise to listen," Sarah said quietly. "You have to promise to listen to everything."

He stuck out his jaw. Shit, he didn't want to listen to how she'd screwed some other guy.

"All of it," she insisted. "From beginning to end." She waved a hand. "I mean, why. Why it happened."

He stared at her. What did she mean, why?

"Promise," she insisted.

His heart ached, because they'd never made each other promise anything before. They'd always just trusted each other. When did that end?

He figured out the answer a moment later. It ended the night he'd told her he was leaving. The night he'd forced him-self to tell her it was over, even though he wanted her more than anything else.

God, what a mess.

"I promise," he said in a choked voice.

Sarah stared a minute longer, then started pacing along the trail at the edge of the lake.

"A little while after you left for the East Coast, my cousin Ginger came to visit. You remember her?"

He scowled, walking alongside her. Yeah, he remembered Ginger. The one with the bad dye job who'd come on to him the second Sarah turned her back. As if he'd be interested in anyone but his mate.

"Ginger said I'd done enough moping about you, and I needed to have some fun. That it was your birthday and you left me alone and you were probably out partying with someone else..."

He scowled deeper. He'd spent that night alone in the woods, longing for his mate.

"...so I should have some fun, too. So she took me to Lafayette. To that techno bar."

He stopped short. "Dart's?"

She nodded.

A thousand alarms went off in his mind. "Jesus, Sarah, don't you know how many women get their drinks spiked there?"

She looked straight at him without saying a word, and his heart sank. Her drink had been spiked while she was there?

"No, I didn't know. Well, I didn't know at the time," she said bitterly.

Well, Soren knew all too well. He'd heard of the place through a friend of a friend. A place to keep clear of, from the sound of it, if guys were slipping women who knew what kind of drug. Not just the usual date rape drugs, but aphrodisiacs, too, according to the rumor mill.

"These guys kept coming on to us, buying us drinks," she started.

Jesus! Todd was supposed to keep an eye out for that kind of thing. Where the hell had Todd been?

"They were totally not my type." Sarah rolled her eyes. "But they were Ginger's type, apparently."

"Ginger," he couldn't help cursing. He'd never liked her.

Sarah gave him a sharp look and spoke in a hushed voice. "Ginger was staying over at my house when it happened — the fire. She died in the fire."

Soren ran a hand through his hair. Shit. It's not like he would wish that on Ginger. Not Ginger, not anyone.

His mind flashed with an image of the smoldering remains of the shop and the body bags being carried out. Three of them, making him think Sarah had died.

"Well, Ginger eventually took off with a guy that night," Sarah said, resuming the story. "The other two guys..." She spoke so quietly, he could barely hear. "Well, I don't know. Somehow, I..."

He clenched his fists to keep his bear claws from breaking out.

"Anyway, the whole thing was a mistake. Ginger went off with one guy, and there were these two other guys and I... I..."

Soren kicked at the ground, scattering gravel.

"God knows what I would have done if Todd hadn't come along—"

His heart screeched to a stop. "Todd?" His cousin and best friend, Todd?

At first, he was elated. Todd had prevented a terrible crime. But then it hit him that Sarah wasn't done with the story yet.

"It was my fault," she said, walking slowly as if in a trance. "He said we shouldn't. Couldn't."

Soren flexed his fingers and clawed at thin air.

"But I pushed him hard enough that he wanted it, too. God, Soren. I missed you so much, and I don't know — with the full moon and the drinks and missing you so much... I wanted you that night more than ever."

He'd wanted her that night, too. Bad enough that he'd jerked off, pretending it was her. And for a while there, he'd convinced himself it was. It felt that real, that good. Until it ended and he was left empty and alone.

"I had my eyes closed the whole time," she said, barely above the breeze.

He squinted at her. She'd always kept her eyes on him, every time they'd been together. Every single time.

"Pretending it was you... For a while, I even believed it was you, touching me. Whispering to me." A tear rolled down her cheek. "And afterward, all I could do was cry, because it felt so wrong."

She walked a few more steps, but Soren stood rooted to the spot as his mind spun.

Not about Todd. Not about spiked drinks. About something completely different.

What was that old legend he'd heard told, long ago? What did they call it?

Moonlust, that was it.

"Moon what?" Sarah spun around.

He hadn't realized he said it aloud, but now he was stuck.

"Moonlust. An old legend." An old *bear* legend, but he left that part out. It happened to mates, they said. The closest, truest destined mates. But how could he tell her that?

"What legend?" she asked, irritated.

"When two people... when two people who are destined to be together think of each other at exactly the same time on exactly the same night, and they... Well, they... "

He let that part hang, because surely she got it by now. When destined mates dreamed themselves right into each other's arms and made a connection that erased the space between them.

"Tell me," he said in a raspy voice. "Tell me what I said to you that night."

She tilted her head at him. "What you said?"

"Tell me what you heard, Sarah." He was speaking too loudly now, and his voice carried across the lake. But it was important. God, everything hinged on what she said next. Had she really heard his thoughts despite all the distance between them that night?

Sarah faced the lake, closed her eyes, and stood silently for so long, he was sure she was never going to speak.

I'll love you forever, my mate, he'd told her that night. That night and that night only, because he'd never risked the word *mate* with her before.

She stooped, picked up a stone, and sent it skipping across the lake. The clouds reflected in the surface scattered and overlapped, suddenly more storm than peaceful afternoon. Fitting

90

for his mood, and for Arizona — a place that could change in the blink of an eye.

Slowly, the blue of the water and the white of the clouds settled back to their respective places again, which meant he was the only one trembling now.

"I'll love you forever, my mate," Sarah whispered. So quietly, he nearly missed it.

Soren stared at her reflection. Stared at the truth, in a way.

Mate, his bear hummed dreamily. *Mate.*

Between the Moonlust and drinks and whatever drug she might have been slipped that night, Sarah had ended up sleeping with Todd. Which was as much his fault as her own, because if he'd worked himself half into a frenzy, imagining he was with her, it would have been the same for Sarah.

Maybe fault isn't the word, his bear said. *Maybe it was destiny.*

Sarah skipped another stone, and Soren stared at the wobbling reflection of the two of them standing side by side. Destiny sure seemed intent on steering them down a twisted path — but to what end? Would it ever let them come together, or would it keep them forever apart?

Chapter Thirteen

Sarah stared at the clouds, rippling across the mirror of the lake, then strode away. She didn't look at Soren. She *couldn't* look at Soren. Her vision blurred as she walked, desperate to escape all the mistakes she'd made. She didn't get far, though, before the gravel next to her crunched and Soren took her gently by the hand.

"Over here," he said in a voice so soft and gentle, she could have cried.

She did cry, all the way over to the bench he led her to. She cried enough to fill a third lake beside the two shining so blue and innocent under the spring sky. Not that she saw much of the scenery between her tears. Mostly, she just saw the past.

She cried and talked, and talked and cried, because now that the dam was broken, she just couldn't stop the deluge. She started from the time Soren departed for the East Coast and babbled on and on, all the way up to the time when she'd wandered into the Quarter Moon Café, not long ago.

And the whole time, Soren held her and stroked her hair and whispered quietly in her ear.

"It'll be okay," he said, over and over. But how could anything be okay after all that had happened?

"Todd started coming around after you left, but I swear we never did anything except that one time. We never even thought about doing anything. He felt as bad about it as I did. I swear. . ."

She shook, just thinking about that crazy night. Her body might have been with Todd, but her heart and mind had been with Soren. God, how different things would be if she'd been more careful.

But somehow, she'd gotten all mixed up and let things go too far. Between the drinks she'd consumed and whatever had come over her, she hadn't exactly been herself. Plus, Todd was so much like Soren — big, strong. Silent. Mysterious, somehow, like all the folks who lived on Soren's side of the mountain.

Soren was special, though. His own type of enigma, with his own broody charm. He'd been her closest friend for years. God, how could she ever have let him let her go? If she'd figured anything out in the past few weeks, it was that something had forced Soren to break up with her. When his eyes locked on hers, they filled with love and laughter and hope. When they drifted out of focus, though, they grew bitter, and he'd glare at something in the past.

Soren held her without saying a word, and she wondered when he'd push her aside and stomp away in anger. But he didn't.

"Then that night... that awful night of the fire..." Her whole body tensed at the memories. "I woke up in bed, smelling the smoke. Thank God I smelled the smoke. But the door was locked, and I couldn't get out. And I couldn't get to my parents because the fire was spreading fast. There were flames everywhere..."

It was all so vivid in her memory — the angry snap of the flames, the steaming hisses, the booming crack as beams collapsed — that she pulled the collar of her shirt up over her mouth as she'd done that night.

Her hands shook as she remembered the heat, the agonizing peeling sensation as the skin of her arms burned.

"I couldn't get my parents or Ginger out. I couldn't get them out," she sobbed. "I couldn't get out of the house, either. The door was barricaded. And outside, there was this circle of men, and I swear they were chanting..."

Soren went tense all over. "Purity. Purity." His tone was flat and quiet, nothing like the dark chant she'd heard, and yet she shuddered, hearing the words again.

"But then Todd drove up—"

"Todd?" For the first time since they got to the bench, Soren's voice was hard.

She gulped, remembering the relief that washed over her when she'd recognized Todd's pickup. "I was about to break a window when he ran up — he ran right through the circle of men — and broke through the door."

"Todd," Soren repeated, all hushed now.

"He saved me, Soren. He saved me."

She squeezed her eyes closed against the memory of Todd taking a stand when the arsonists closed in on them.

"He yelled at me to run for the car, and he fought the men to give me a chance. Jesus, did he fight."

Soren stiffened and went dead quiet.

"I got to the car and tried to drive to him, but then they were on him..." She trailed off as the awful vision replayed in her mind. Of Todd, falling out of sight. Of the gang of men, hammering down at him with fists and bats and stones.

"I left him there," she cried. "I left him and my parents and saved my own skin."

"Sarah, you had no choice."

"I should have tried something."

She protested until Soren practically shook her. "You had no choice. Jess and Janna had to do the same thing."

Then he was the one who was hunched and shaking, holding his head in his hands while she hugged him tighter than she ever had before.

"I should have been there," he said. "I could have fought them..."

"Then you would have died, too. There were too many. Dozens." She'd even imagined seeing wolves prance around the flames, but she wasn't about to share that.

She held Soren, and Soren held her. She cried a little longer. Well, a lot longer, until the tears dried up and he patted her hair.

"Did Todd know? About the baby?"

She could have shed another gallon of tears about that, but she was all cried out by then. She shook her head and spoke hoarsely.

95

"He didn't know. I didn't even know. Not then, I didn't. God. He didn't know."

It felt so unjust. So wrong that a man who'd never been anything but good to her — a friend who died for her — wouldn't ever know about his own child. A child he hadn't planned on any more than she had.

Then her muddled mind twitched with another thought. She sat up quickly with a hand on her stomach.

"Oh! The baby!"

"What?" Soren grabbed her arm.

"The doctor...the doctor saw something wrong."

He blew out a breath. "There's nothing wrong with the baby, Sarah."

How could he know? How could he be sure?

"But...but..."

He took a deep breath and took hold of both of her hands. "My turn to talk to you."

"About what?" She narrowed her eyes at him, wondering what he could possibly say to put her mind at ease.

He scraped a hand through his hair, mesmerizing her as sunlight shone through the golden brown. He leaned forward like a man on the cusp of a major revelation, and she held her breath.

A raven cawed, and her head snapped around. Not so much at the bird, but at growing aware of her surroundings again. Everything was peaceful and calm, but the hair on the back of her neck stood.

"What?" Soren asked, looking around.

She shivered. There it was again — that feeling of being watched. Of danger closing in. Not as close as she'd felt it before, when she'd grabbed the first bus she could catch and fled an invisible foe. But still, the lunatics who wanted her dead were out there, and they were hunting her down. Or maybe they were simply thinking of setting out to hunt her down, because the feeling passed a minute later.

"What is it?" Soren asked.

She stood up, taking his hand. "Nothing. Probably nothing. But let's get home, okay?"

Soren's brow went from being tightly knitted to smooth, and his eyes lit up when she said that.

"Home?"

She squeezed his hand. God, did they have a lot to figure out. But right now...

She managed a thin smile at the thought. "Home."

She held his hand all through the drive back to the saloon, and that itchy, crawling feeling of being watched dissipated bit by bit. Maybe it was having the solid bulk of Soren at her side that did it. Maybe it was the feeling of coming home or of being greeted so casually by the others, as if she truly belonged. Whatever it was, her soul warmed, and the creeping feeling of being watched was gone.

The minute they returned to the saloon, Soren was called off to a meeting with Ty Hawthorne — the man whose family leased the saloon to the Voss brothers. And though her heart ached to see Soren go, his absence did present an opportunity to get back to work on the saloon accounts, because it ate at her, just imagining the mess. She spent the whole afternoon in the office, shaking her head and muttering. But she enjoyed it, too — running her hands over the armrest of Soren's chair, just where his arms would go. Inhaling the faint traces of Soren's oaky scent along with the leathery fragrance of the desk blotter and the scent of wood oil in the air. The office might not be a good place for Soren, but it reminded her of him.

Jessica fed her double portions at dinner, and Janna even got her to play a round of pool, which wasn't easy with the baby in the way. But it was fun. Casual. Relaxed in a way she hadn't felt in ages.

Soren still wasn't back, so she squeezed in another hour of work after that, letting the scents of the office surround her with memories, just the way the sheets of her bed did when she finally called it a day. Headlights passed outside the window at intervals, and she wondered which might belong to Soren's truck. Her heart thumped a little harder when she heard his heavy footsteps coming up the stairs. But there was no knock at her door, no whisper. Just a pause in which she could imagine Soren lifting a hand to knock, then shaking his head and moving on.

Soren! She wanted to call out. *Come to me.*

The footsteps continued to the bathroom, then backtracked to his room.

She lay staring at the ceiling, telling herself to sleep. But she couldn't. Just like so many other nights of the past few weeks, she lay there, wishing for him. Wanting him. Needing him even more desperately than before.

She ran her hands over her stomach, pretending they were his. And though it started as a soft, innocent touch, her hands started roving to places that were far from innocent. Was it the hormones of pregnancy making her horny tonight, or was it pent-up need finally coming out?

Either way, she was like a cat in heat, and she needed release, soon.

The curtains rippled quietly on a zephyr of a breeze, and she caught a glimpse of the crescent moon hanging low in the sky, just above the rooftops across the street.

She traced the same shape around her breasts and thought about what Soren had said. What had he called it? Moon. . . moon. . .

Moonlust. His words echoed in her mind. *When two people who are destined to be together think of each other at exactly the same time on exactly the same night. . .*

She smiled, remembering Soren saying the words. A man of few words could be a poet sometimes.

"Moonlust," she whispered out loud. Maybe she should try it out sometime.

Maybe she should try it out right now.

She slid her hands over her breasts, and her nipples peaked. God, what she'd give for Soren to come prowling into her room right now. She was fed up with being lonely. She was fed up with curling up alone. Fed up with pretending she didn't feel the same spark she'd always had for Soren.

A spark that blazed into a raging inferno until she was burning with need.

She'd always figured jacking off was for guys, but heck, if the Moonlust thing didn't work, at least she might ease a little of the itch. So she slid her hands slowly up her torso and lifted her breasts, the way she wanted Soren to. Scooped the soft, pliant flesh and circled them this way and that. She closed her eyes and tipped her head back, pretending it was him.

Yes, that was good. She teased herself the way he would, pulling her hands away, then letting them sneak back, and her body grew hotter and hotter. Her need grew wilder until she was pumping her hips in time to the motion of her hands over her breasts. She caught a nipple and twirled her fingers around it, making it harden and rise. It was like an on button, and her legs danced under the sheets as if they were tangling with his.

Soren. Soren.

"Soren." She called to him, in her mind and in a whisper, touching herself the whole time. She closed her eyes and pictured him moving over her. He'd slide a hand between her knees and trace the inner curve up...

"Soren," she moaned, already burning with anticipation. Anticipation and frustration, because it was just a mirage.

She imagined a knock on the door. Imagined it opening and Soren standing there, watching her touch herself. Would he like that? Or would he chuckle and tell her she was doing it wrong?

The ceiling fan turned slowly, and she pictured him entering the room. He'd step around the mattress and go to the window first. After a quick glance outside, he'd open it wider and throw the curtains back so the moon wasn't just peeking around the corner but shining right in.

Her eyes were closed, but she tipped her head toward the window, imagining Soren standing there, fists clenched at his sides as he watched her. His erection would grow stiffer and stand higher as he watched her. She pictured that long, thick shaft filling her. Sliding in and out as the friction increased. It would build and build until he pounded into her with long, hard strokes, giving her the high she craved. He'd rock her higher and higher until she soared among the stars, then rasp her name, and he'd—

"Sarah," Soren whispered as the door squeaked open, two steps away.

She kept perfectly still, wondering what he might do.

"Sarah," Soren repeated in a voice husky with need.

She turned her head to the door, and there he stood. Not backlit by moonlight, but with the same clenched fists and the same jutting erection she'd imagined. The same need punctuating his voice.

She stretched her hand toward him, wondering if it was an illusion that might waver and disappear.

"Come to me, my love," she whispered in the half darkness. "Come to me."

Chapter Fourteen

Soren tried to keep his breath steady, but the minute she said the words, his heart leaped.

Come to me, my love.

Mate, his bear called to her. *My mate.*

His whole body called to her like hers called to him, and he turned his brain off. Hell, he'd turned it off a while ago when he'd lain naked in bed, tossing and turning and thinking of her. Not about the baby, not about the news Ty Hawthorne had shared with him, not about the saloon.

Her. Everything ceased to exist except her. All that was left was the burning need. Wrapping his own hands around his aching cock was no good. He needed her.

It was like all the other nights he'd dreamed of Sarah — with the need turned up by a factor of ten or twenty or more. He could hear her whispering in his ear, imagine her touching herself.

She needed him, too. He could sense her desperate desire.

She's right there, his bear had urged him. *Right in the next room. Not in your dreams. Not in heaven. She's right there.*

Sarah was a few steps away, touching herself and wishing for him. He could feel it. See it. Sense it as if those were his hands exploring her bare flesh. So what the hell was he doing, lying in his room, all alone?

How he hadn't tripped over his own feet in his rush to get to her door, he didn't know, but there he was. And more importantly, there she was, beckoning to him.

"Soren," she whispered again. "Come to me, my love."

She loved him! She wanted him!

She always has, his bear reprimanded him. *Just like we love her.*

Every muscle in his body twitched for her, but when he stepped into her room and closed the door behind him, he headed for the window first. Instinct led him there to let in the cool night air, along with a little bit of moonlight. He didn't stoop to look, but he knew the stars of the Great Bear were out there, too, shining on him.

He pushed back the curtains and looked at Sarah for a long minute, balling his hands into fists. He itched to touch her, to kiss her, to fill her, but he needed to watch, too.

"Sarah," he whispered across the room, because he could. Because she was really there.

"Soren," she breathed. The sheets were a mess, and he could see her knee sticking up on one side and one bare breast peeking out the other side.

God, he could admire that view forever.

Her hand rubbed over her breast, and he watched the tight nipple rise. He could practically taste it between his lips, feel the tiny bumps around it on his tongue.

Sarah started circling her breast just as his hand wrapped around his cock, and they both watched each other breathlessly.

"This is crazy," she mumbled.

"Crazy?" Yes, he'd been crazy to ever let her go. But watching her like this felt just right.

"All this time apart, and what are we doing now that we're finally together?"

His mind skipped and replayed her words, packing in a thousand echoes in the pause that followed. *Now that we're finally together...*

"What?" he gulped.

"Watching." She shook her head.

"I like watching you."

"I like watching you, too. But I like feeling you even more."

His chest rose with a huge lungful of air he savored along with the words. The room was thick with the scent of her desire.

"I can feel you," he insisted.

She tilted her head.

"Close your eyes." He saw the protest on the tip of her tongue and hurried on. "Just for a second, close your eyes."

He watched that she'd done it, then let his eyelids drop. "Now, feel," he whispered.

He sent his mind out to tap hers and let his body replay her movements. How her fingers opened and closed and curved around her breast...

"Soren..."

"Shh. Just feel."

He imagined it was her hand, wrapped around his cock, and his fingers, playing over her breast. So soft, so perfect. He touched one, then the other, and lowered his head to kiss. To lick, too. He imagined the moon shining on her skin, and it felt so real, so incredibly good...

Moonlust, his bear gave a dreamy nod.

"Soren..." Sarah called, but it wasn't a protest this time. It was a moan. "So good..."

When he squeezed his lips tighter around her nipple and pinched the other side harder, he could feel her rise against him and her hand tighten around his cock. The boundaries blurred until it didn't matter who was touching whom any more, because he could feel himself and feel her at the same time. He could feel her pleasure and her building need.

She pumped down to the base of his cock, then slid up and played with the velvety tip, driving him crazy in the very best way.

"Soren," she called, and his hand slid toward her sex. Her hand, actually, but it felt like his.

Touch her! his bear called just loud enough to break him out of the spell. *Take her!*

His eyes snapped open exactly as hers did, and they watched each other pant for five or six heartbeats.

"Wow," she breathed.

He nodded. It had been so real.

She rolled sideways and reached out her hand. "You. I need you. Not just in my imagination."

A faint hallelujah chorus filled the corners of his mind.

She held up the edge of the sheet, and two steps later, he slid into place like they'd choreographed exactly that move a thousand times. And of course, they had in the past, but not quite this way. There was the baby to work around this time, but somehow, he knew exactly where to go, just how to fit. One arm over here, one leg along hers over there, and his mouth...

The second his lips closed over hers, he consumed them. Devoured them. He reached deeper and deeper until she was whimpering with pleasure. All the need pent up over a year of abstinence and sorrow came pouring out — his and hers like two waves moving in opposite directions and coming together with a crash. He came up for a breath of air, and suddenly, it was her, pushing him onto the mattress and engulfing him with a hundred hungry kisses and licks. Her tongue danced with his, and she made desperate little noises that drove his bear wild. So wild, he jackknifed up and rolled, rearing above her again.

I like feeling you, she'd said.

He'd let her feel him, all right. He hung on to the kiss until his lungs burned, and after a quick breath of air, he moved down her body to her breasts. The left side. God, the right side. Both so, so good. Soft and malleable yet hard in the center where her nipples practically begged for his mouth. He sucked on one, much harder and longer than in the vision they'd shared, and Sarah writhed beneath him. Her hands were everywhere, igniting separate fires everywhere they came down — fires that spread and blended until his bear roared for more.

Mate! his bear crowed wildly. *Mine!*

"Yes...ahh..."

God, he loved the noises she made.

He feasted on her taste, her scent, her soft skin. Wondered how the hell he'd survived as long as he had without her and why he'd ever thought he could. And when he slipped a hand lower to trace the folds of her sex, his ears just about exploded from the rush of blood through his veins. Or maybe it was Moonlust, letting him feel the rush in *her* veins.

104

He swept his finger deeper, making her buck and moan.

He didn't say much because he couldn't say much. He just thought it over and over.

Love you. Love you. Love you.

Want to make you mine, his bear added in a growly undertone. *Make you mine.*

His gums ached from where his bear teeth pushed, trying to extend, ready for a mating bite. He'd fought the same urge off a thousand times before, but it was harder than ever this time. This time, he knew what he was risking. He knew it was crazy to assume he'd have another chance. If he didn't take her now...

But if he did take her now, he'd be betraying the trust he was only barely starting to win back. Sarah didn't know about shifters. She didn't know about the mating bite.

She'd want it! his bear cried. *She'd agree!*

He could have snorted. Like a bear could judge. Like he could judge in the state he was in.

No. Tonight was not for mating or confessing or explaining. It was to reunite. To learn her body all over again. To try to make things up to her. To make her sing with pleasure.

"Soren," she cried as he touched deeper.

That was the song. That was what he wanted to hear.

He ran two fingers through her folds, then dipped in.

"God, Soren..."

She was warm and slippery and so, so ready for him.

He turned his head from one nipple to the other while circling his fingers inside her.

"Oh, yes..."

She danced on his hand and under his mouth. Her fingers raked his hair. Her hips rose right off the bed.

"So good..."

It was more than good. It was heaven. All these months, he'd been a ghost. Now, he was alive. Blissfully, joyously alive, because he had his mate.

Her chest lifted as she tipped her head back and cried out. She was so, so close, but stubbornly holding out at the same time. Every muscle in her body was wound incredibly tight.

Her nails clawed at his shoulders as she sought out a new position.

"You," she panted. "Need you inside. Please, Soren." She twisted and rolled.

He rolled, too, in another one of those perfect moments that some outside hand seemed to be guiding them through like a couple of puppets on strings. She rose up, taking the top as he stretched on his back. She split into a straddle and gazed down at him with wild, hungry eyes.

Her mouth opened with words she didn't utter as she slid along his body, seeking his cock. He guided her hips higher, gritting his teeth as the ache in his cock increased. He was so close to entering her. So close to home.

She pushed down exactly when he thrust up, and for a moment, they both froze there, practically in midair. Her whole face went slack with ecstasy, and her mouth opened in a silent *Oh.*

Sweet and tight and hot, her body swallowed him up, and her head tipped back as she began to rock, riding him with long, slow strokes of her hips. Her eyes were half closed, her mouth open, and the sounds that escaped her were music to his ears.

"Yes..."

She went faster, taking him deeper. Leaning farther and farther back until the angle was perfect and his cock seated sinfully deep.

Her hair swayed with her shoulders, and her perfect breasts danced just above his eyes. The baby bump rested on his stomach, not at all the issue he thought it might be. He wrapped his fingers around her hips and stretched his thumbs as far toward her center as he could, strumming one and then the other against her clit.

Sarah cried with every breath she took.

"So good..." she croaked, driving her whole body against his.

His cock burned. Ached. Begged, but he sure as hell wasn't coming until she did. But damn, it would be close. He thrust harder and tweaked his thumbs faster, rushing over the last steps to an awe-inspiring peak in exact time with her. They teetered on the edge, and Sarah shuddered and moaned.

He closed his eyes as release hit him like a flash of white lightning, and for a moment, pleasure burned through him. It burned through her, too, and he swore he could feel that just as well. How good she felt. How deep he was, almost a part of her.

When she dropped down beside him, going from taut to beautifully limp, a cottony blanket of bliss washed over him.

"Soren," she panted into the skin of his neck. "Soren..."

Mine, he mumbled, sweeping his arms around her to hold her close. *Mine.*

Chapter Fifteen

Sarah all but melted into the sheets, trying to catch her breath. Not caring too much that she couldn't because all that really mattered was staying close to Soren. Warmth washed over her, and a crazy little leftover current shot through her body, lighting up her nerves.

It had been so long since she'd touched him. So long since she'd felt this good, this safe.

She was about to say something when her body shuddered with an aftershock of pure pleasure.

"Yes..." she moaned as Soren tightened his hold on her. Jesus, the man wasn't even in her any more, and he could still make her high. "Oh..."

It was yet another one of those times when she wanted to say everything but couldn't manage anything, and yet Soren seemed to understand. Calm, quiet Soren, the man who listened more than he talked. When he cuddled her closer and ran a finger over her lips, his impossibly clear blue eyes shone brighter than ever.

"What are you looking at?" she asked, gazing up at him with what had to be the world's goofiest smile.

He smiled one of those rare Soren smiles that was more than just upturned lips — it was bunched-up cheeks and shining eyes and a hazy kind of inner glow.

"You," he said quietly. "You."

Then he dipped his head and proceeded to nuzzle her halfway into the mattress, scrubbing his stubble up and down her neck, her cheeks, her chin. He rubbed from one sensitive spot to another, and every part of her that had forgotten about joy and hope over the past few months suddenly came back to life. Her skin begged for mercy, but her soul wanted more. More of the close contact, the intimacy. The *I love you, I need you, I want you* buried under every long scrape of his chin. Words she even imagined hearing in her head.

I love you, Soren, she nearly replied. *Need you. Want you, too.*

They lay gazing into each other's eyes, and she didn't know whether to measure the time in minutes or hours. Whenever his eyes roamed over her naked body, they didn't seem to snag on her protruding belly the way they once had.

When the baby shifted, she nearly panicked, because his eyes went wide.

God, this was it. The magic spell — the Moonlust — that had bound him to her was about to burst. She braced herself, waiting for him to frown and roll away.

But Soren didn't frown. He didn't roll away. He just looked at her with a question in his eyes. His hand slid along the sheets, closer to her stomach, and she held her breath.

Can I touch? his raised eyebrows asked.

A funny question coming from a man who'd just touched every part of her body in the most intimate way possible. But yes, this was different. Completely different, the way opening a diary was different than opening a notebook.

She bit her lip, knotted her fingers through his, and rested all four of their hands on her belly.

The baby turned a little more, and Soren's mouth cracked open. His hand flattened against her skin, and the breath he'd been holding came out in a long, even sigh. He watched intently for another minute, then stroked her skin with one thumb.

If Sarah hadn't already cried a river that day, she might not have blinked her tears back. But even if they were tears of joy and relief, she'd had enough crying for a day. For a lifetime, really.

"Hey," she whispered.

He looked up with shining eyes. "Hey."

Not exactly poetry, but coming from Soren...

She smiled and tugged on his shoulders, bringing him face-to-face for another kiss. His lips were dry on the outside, soft on the inside. She skimmed the perfect line of his teeth with her tongue, and damn it, there she went, making hungry cat noises all over again.

Her hips pushed against his, and she wrapped a leg around his calf.

"Mmm," he murmured in a *Hungry already?* kind of way.

Of course, she was hungry for him. They had a hell of a lot of lost loving to make up for.

"Mmm," she mumbled, nodding through the next kiss.

They lay side by side, and a shockingly calculating part of her mind raced ahead to their options. They'd just done her-on-top, and she'd been breathless knowing it was a rare instance of Soren surrendering control of anything to anyone. But the cat-in-heat urge building in her demanded something hotter. Harder.

"This way," she whispered, turning her back to him.

Soren sucked in a quick breath, like he'd been waiting for just that chance. He pulled her tighter, keeping her back to his chest. They were still on their sides, now both facing the window.

His breath tickled her ear, and he looped an arm over her side. He dropped kisses on her shoulder and stroked her ribs, then the underside of her breasts.

"Mmm. Nice." She exhaled, arching into him.

"Nice," he agreed, teasing her nipples into tight peaks.

"Nice," she mumbled, pushing her rear back into his groin.

The hard length of him jutted up against her tailbone, and her body practically cried for satisfaction.

Once Soren had the reins, though, the ride was all his, and he wasn't quite ready to let her gallop away.

"Patience," he growled in her ear. His hand slipped lower, gently guiding her legs apart.

"Patience?" she panted as he teased her folds.

A *just-watch-this* grunt came from over her shoulder as he circled her clit, then rubbed her entrance with the flat of his palm. His big, broad hand teased her, driving her wild.

She moaned, and he kissed her shoulder, telling her he liked that, so she let herself do it again. Not enough to alert the whole neighborhood, but enough to let him know how she felt.

"God, Soren. How am I supposed to be patient when you— Oh!" she cried out as two thick fingers warmed her inside.

She couldn't help but rock against his hand, relishing the feel of his arousal against her body. She tilted her head back, desperate for his nipping kisses.

"Here," he whispered, guiding her hand to her nipple and rolling it together with her. His fingers were slippery from touching her inside, and once he got her going at her own breast, he drew a line down her side and went right back to toying with her sex. He scissored his fingers inside her then circled and pumped.

"God, Soren. . ." she whimpered over and over, about to come undone.

He wasn't that far off, either, judging by the tension building behind her. When he finally whispered in her ear, she was all too happy to oblige.

"Like this," he said, helping her get to all fours.

Yes, yes, yes! her body cried, feeling him come up behind her.

One callused hand toyed with her swaying breasts, then dragged her hips back against his, and when he thrust forward—

"Yes!" she cried.

He withdrew, then rammed back, and her whole body pitched forward.

"Too hard?" he asked through clenched teeth.

She panted, ramming back against him. "I want hard."

He withdrew far enough to nearly break contact, then pushed back in.

"Harder," she breathed, dropping her head.

He pulled out, waited just long enough to torture her, then burst back in with a grunt.

"Harder," she cried.

The deeper he reached, the more she craved him, and her cries grew more and more desperate. He drove her higher and higher. Physically higher, too, working her up the mattress in heated spurts that made her crazy with desire.

"So good," she croaked as his steady rhythm tipped over into a frenzy. Anchoring her elbows on the bed, she pushed back against him, countering each thrust until they were both panting and groaning and urging each other on.

He took hold of her left hip to help her push back, and she squeezed her eyes shut against the beautiful friction building inside.

"Yes. . . yes. . . "

She *yesed* him through four more thrusts and the long, shuddering high that overcame both of them a second later.

"Yes." Even Soren succumbed to the need to moan something at the peak of the ride. He held her tight against his body as he came inside her.

"So good," she whispered a second later.

Panting into a pillow with her ass in the air shouldn't qualify as the most glorious high of her life, but she was pretty sure it was. They'd had sex so many times in the past, but this was different. It was raw and a little rough. Possessive, and though she hated to admit it, she needed that. God, she needed that.

"Sarah," he whispered in a way that suggested he still couldn't believe it was her.

Then she was melting again, and it was all she could do to slide around and clean up with a corner of the sheet — a mess she'd feel guilty about later. Right now, all she wanted was Soren.

He scooped her against the curve of his chest, and there they were, back where they'd started. They kept their hands wrapped around each other, and their chests rose and fell in perfect time.

She stared hazily across the dim room. The crescent moon was higher now, a sliver of light in the upper corner of the window that smiled at her.

"Goodnight," she whispered, more to the moon than to Soren.

"Goodnight," he echoed, kissing her skin.

Chapter Sixteen

Two days passed, and in that time, Soren went from a soaring high to the lowest low.

"You really need to tell her," Janna nagged as they got ready to open the saloon.

It was one of those warm spring afternoons in high-altitude Arizona where the shade felt just right and a cold drink even better. Warm without being overly hot; dry without being painful on the skin. Peaceful, in a way, because the town slowed down just like flies did when they'd had too much sun.

"Come on, Soren. When are you going to tell her?"

He thumped down a crate of beer. The longer he waited, the harder it would be to tell her, and the more he was being dishonest to Sarah. But Jesus, how do you tell a woman her unborn baby was a bear shifter? How?

He could just see it now.

Sarah, your baby is a shifter.

A what?

A bear shifter. But it'll be really cute, I promise.

He swore out loud. He'd have to explain that he was a bear, too.

Oh, and by the way, everyone else in the apartment is a shifter, too. You've been surrounded by bears and wolves all this time. Sorry I never bothered to tell you.

He blew out a long puff of air.

"That's not going to help," Simon murmured as he walked by.

No, it wasn't, but what the hell would he say? When? How?

115

Simon knew that he'd started sleeping with Sarah again. Hell, everyone knew, because the scent of sex was unmistakable — not to mention that he'd gone and marked her thoroughly by scrubbing his own scent into her skin with his chin each time. He might not be able to mark her with a mating bite—

Yet, his bear filled in.

—but he sure as hell couldn't hold back from nuzzling her half into giggles each night.

He smiled, thinking about it. Hearing Sarah laugh, seeing her smile... Another light in the darkness of his soul turned on every time she showed her joy. It was like someone had finally bought the dilapidated old house at the end of town that everyone said was haunted and started renovating it, one room at a time.

So, yeah, everyone knew, and everyone nagged him to tell Sarah, though none of them had any bright ideas on how. And why should they? Simon's mate was a born shifter, so he never had to explain to Jess. A wound had already started Cole down the road to turning shifter when Janna fell in love with him, so it wasn't as if he had a choice. None of them faced what Soren had to do now.

And shit, Sarah didn't have much choice either, did she? The baby was coming. Soon.

So he wasn't exactly in a good mood to begin with, and it only got worse when Ty Hawthorne, alpha of Twin Moon pack, pulled into the saloon's back lot. Lana, Ty's mate, was there, too, along with about fifteen other rough, tough shifters in five or six vehicles that parked not very discreetly down the alley.

Something was going down. He could feel it in the air. These were shifters on the move. Shifters with a mission.

"We've got word Whyte and the Blue Bloods are heading south," Ty said. Quietly, so no one else would hear. "We're going after him."

Soren's first reaction was, *Great, let me tell the others, and I'll be right out.*

But Ty stuck a hand on his chest and fixed him with that laser glare. "You're staying."

For a minute, he couldn't even answer. Couldn't speak. Anger welled up in him and roared in his ears.

"The hell I'm staying."

Ty shook his head. "You're staying."

A growl built in his chest and filled in the hard edges around his words. "The Blue Bloods killed my clan. My clan!" His voice cracked when he barked the words, damn it. How dare Ty suggest he stay home?

You're staying, the alpha's dark eyes ordered one more time.

Two words — a death sentence for his soul. Going after the Blue Bloods was his right. His responsibility. He and his brother had tracked and taken out dozens of guilty rogues in the wake of the massacre in Montana, but they'd never managed to get their hands on Whyte, the one who'd ordered the attack.

"Whyte is mine," he growled.

Simon appeared at his side. The minute he heard the news, hair popped out all over his arms as his fury brought him close to shifting.

"What the hell do you mean, we're not coming?"

Ty kept up that unwavering gaze. "We need to keep level heads when we move in. Take out the leaders but figure out who deserves to live."

"My family deserved to live!" Soren practically yelled, right in the face of the most powerful shifter in the Four Corners area.

Everyone he'd ever loved and lost might as well have marched down the street just then — one sorely missed friend and relative after another. The faces, the quirks of each of them felt that real, the loss that gutting. He'd shoved the memories into the farthest reaches of his mental closet for all these months. Never really given himself the chance to mourn or remember good times along with the bad. But now they jumped out at him, all those mournful faces asking him why he hadn't been there to fight for them.

"They didn't kill your mother. Your father," he hissed at Ty. "They didn't take each and every person in your family and burn them aliv—"

It was Simon who dragged him back and forced him to get his shit together. And it was Lana, Ty's mate, who stepped forward and put a hand on his arm.

"Soren, I know it's hard. But if you were Ty and he were you, what decision would you make? Who would you bring?"

I'd take me, he wanted to scream, but he knew she was right. He'd leave anyone whose emotions might get in the way at a critical moment. The important thing was to wipe out Whyte before he spread his ugly gospel through more of the shifter world, not who did the dirty work.

But damn did he want to be the one to rip that asshole limb from limb.

He bared his teeth and grunted — not at Ty or Lana, but at fate. Fate, coming to deal him yet another blow.

He could hear a voice laughing on the wind. *Ha! Got you again.*

"Cut it out," his brother told him, reading his mind. Then he turned to Ty. "Get those bastards. Get every one."

As the wolves drove off, Soren hung his head and spit the bitterness out of his mouth. Tried to, anyway. Christ, he'd never find peace. Never. Not like this. They really expected him to sit around at home while they did his dirty work?

He stared at his feet. Yep. They did.

"Fuck." He kicked at the asphalt.

Simon left him and got back to work. And Soren... Well, what choice did he have?

Sarah was napping upstairs, and he itched to go lie down next to her and tank up on some of the soothing energy he got just from being close to her. But he couldn't go bug her with rage and frustration seeping off him like a bad smell. She needed to rest. The two of them had been staying up much too late at night, and she'd been waking up early to open the café, though she always did it with a smile. Always with a smile.

So the least he could do was paste on something less than a frown and get to work, right?

But then Janna started on him again, and the last little bit of his self-control blew.

"I'll tell Sarah about shifters if you don't," she said, flipping the last of the upturned chairs to the floor, ready for opening time.

Of course, Janna didn't know what had just happened in the back lot. Janna didn't know how short his fuse was just then. But he exploded all the same.

"Enough!" he roared so loudly, the glasses behind the bar shook. "I will not tell you again. Enough!"

If Simon hadn't yanked the bottle of whiskey out of his hand, he'd have flung it through the window to punctuate his point.

Janna turned white, then red, then glared at him, but she kept her mouth shut. Everyone went silent until the only sound was his ragged breath and the quiet whir of the ceiling fan.

What a dick, the fan seemed to squeak. *What a dick.*

Janna didn't talk to him for the rest of the night. Simon barely did, either. Jess was the only one who even met his eyes, and when she did, she looked sad and speechless.

God, he really was a dick. He'd shown his teeth and yelled like a real bastard of an alpha. He felt terrible about it all night, not that that changed anything.

"I'm out of here," Janna said at midnight, when Cole pulled up in his truck outside, straight from a late meeting at Seymour Ranch.

"Where are you going?" Jess asked.

"Cole and I are going dancing."

Soren nearly snorted. Dancing. Just great. But cleanup was done, and Janna was an adult, and yes, she deserved to have a good time tonight.

Simon finished cleaning up behind the bar, grabbed his car keys, and slipped an arm over Jessica's shoulders. "See you," he said.

Soren stared for a second. His brother was leaving him, too?

"We're going out." Simon looked at Jess with a weary smile. "Time to let the bear out for a little run."

Great. Just fucking great. His brother and Jess were going for a midnight romp in the woods. Janna and Cole were dancing. The wolves of Twin Moon Ranch were out hunting the murderer he despised. And Soren. . .

Soren leaned back against the bar and shook his head.

"You'll be okay?" Jess asked softly.

Sure. Just fucking great, he wanted to say. But he'd done enough barking tonight.

He nodded. "Fine."

Their footsteps carried out the door and down the street, and a moment later, a car fired up and drove away.

Soren turned around, and he let his eyes travel every inch of the bar he'd worked so hard on, months back. Well, he studied every part except the mirror, because he didn't have the stomach to face himself right now. He felt a thousand years old and probably looked it, too.

He tilted his head back, raising his eyes from the glittering bottles and varnished oak shelves, past the finely carved supports. Lamplight glinted off the barrel of the 1873 Winchester he'd restored and hung there, and shadows played over the scene carved in the upper portion of the bar. A wolf howled at the moon, and a bear waded in a stream, while an eagle soared above them.

He'd never understood wolves' love of howling at the moon, but damn, he'd never been so close to trying it as he was tonight.

He sighed at all the work he'd put into that bar. All the hours, all the sawdust in his nostrils. He'd been so proud, but shit. Fixing up that bar might turn out to be the sole accomplishment of his life.

Soren Voss, alpha of Blue Moon clan, going down in history for nothing more than *that.*

He poured himself a stiff drink and spent a long time wiping glasses that didn't need to be wiped, staring off into nothingness. Didn't bother closing the front door, because the swinging saloon doors let in the cool night air. The voice of fate floated in and cackled at him from time to time. That or the sound of a late-night driver out on the street.

An hour passed that way, or maybe two, and he was just about to pour himself another bourbon — a dangerous move for a man with far too many bottles within arm's reach — when footsteps hurried down the creaky stairs in the back.

"Soren?"

He thumped the bottle down and pushed away the glass. Why did Sarah sound so panicked?

"What's wrong?" he stepped out to intercept her, but she swept right past him and peered out over the saloon doors, leaning forward in the sneakers she'd slipped over bare feet.

She'd taken to wearing one of his old T-shirts as a night-gown, and it fell just high enough on her thighs to capture his gaze for a little too long. God, she was beautiful, with her long legs, red hair, and willowy figure. But why did she sound so scared?

He put an arm over her shoulders and looked up and down the street. "What's wrong?"

You have to tell her, his bear insisted. *Tell her about me.*

As if that would settle whatever had her nerves so frayed.

She shivered, so he pulled her closer. "I felt it again. That, *they're coming for me* feeling..."

He didn't have to ask who *they* were. He knew. But Sarah was wrong. Ty Hawthorne was ferreting out the Blue Bloods somewhere miles away. Annihilating them, if all went according to plan.

Tell her! his bear insisted.

Jesus, now was hardly the time.

He wrapped her in his arms and inhaled deeply through her hair. "It's good. It's all good. You're safe here. The baby is safe here."

She hugged him tight, but periodic shivers still shook her thin frame.

He held her close and rocked her, almost in an extra-slow dance in the last fading beats of a song, and a little bit of peace settled over him again. He kissed the top of her head and ran his arms up and down her back.

"See? Nothing to worry about here—"

Alarms rang out from the fire house two blocks down, and Sarah's head snapped up.

"Fire?"

They both stepped out onto the sidewalk and looked at the bustle of activity down the street.

He wanted to shrug it off and tell Sarah it was just a fire, but *just* and *fire* didn't seem like a good combination to try on a woman who'd survived what she had.

"Quick! Quick! Help! Anyone!" a desperate voice cried, and a man ran up the other end of the street.

Soren spun around.

"Oh, God. No," Sarah murmured, pointing to the shop front across the street. The reflection in the windows showed flames rising over rooftops from a building a few blocks behind the saloon.

"Quick! Help!" the man yelled, rushing to them. He grabbed Soren's arm. "We need to get them out!"

Soren didn't know who was stuck, but he sure wasn't going to waste time talking.

"Wait here," he said, stepping away from Sarah.

"But—"

"Please!" the man pleaded, yanking on his arm. "There are people trapped in there!"

He glanced at the fire house. The fire trucks hadn't even rolled out yet; they might be too late.

He looked at Sarah, and his heart screamed, *Don't leave her! Don't go!*

But how could he not go? How could he not help?

Summoning all the resolve he had, he wheeled away from her and sprinted down the street.

Chapter Seventeen

"Wait, Soren!" Sarah called, but he was already gone with the man who'd begged for help.

She watched him race down the sidewalk, then disappear around a right turn.

She leaned against the outside wall of the saloon and wrapped her arms around herself, watching the reflection of the flames dance in the shop windows across the street. God, not another fire. Not another life lost. And God, please, not Soren. She couldn't lose him, too.

Of course, he was right to try to help. But she prayed the fire department would get there first, because they were the experts and they were well equipped. But Jesus, what was taking them so long?

The fire was somewhere behind the saloon, and though she could have run out back or crossed the street to see the fire directly, the reflection was bad enough. Her right hand brushed over the left, and the left over the right in a nervous washing motion as she remembered the searing pain of her burns.

She clamped her hands together. Praying would probably help as much as worrying did, but what else could she do?

Please, God. Please don't take another life.

Frantic figures ran by. People emerged from buildings to see what was going on and shouted. Sirens sounded as two fire trucks blazed down the street in a blur of noise and flashing red lights. They swung around the corner just as Soren had done.

"Fire!" people shouted. "Fire!"

She shivered, telling herself it was the chill in the air or the fire, not the creeping feeling she'd awoken to. That feeling that the evil she thought she'd finally evaded was back.

She looked one way down the street, then the other. Streets that had grown eerily quiet while the action shifted to the scene of the fire. There were shadows everywhere...

Shadows that didn't rush by. Shadows that watched. Waited.

A cold chill sliced down her spine. She backed toward the saloon doors. Something was wrong. Something more than the fire.

Soren! she screamed in her mind.

A figure separated itself from the darkness and started walking calmly down the middle of the street toward the saloon. A tall man, clad all in black. A second man joined him, wearing a suit that was somehow more sinister for being a pure, clean white.

They weren't heading for the fire. They were heading for her with a cocky assurance that put ice in her blood.

Just like in her nightmares, she opened her mouth, but no sound came out.

Get inside! Lock the door! she screamed at her own feet, but they seemed mired in mud.

Seconds ticked by, and all she could do was stare while several more shadows appeared along the block and started an eerie chant.

"Purity. Purity..."

Something in her finally snapped, and she stumbled through the saloon doors. They squeaked back and forth on their hinges as she reached up frantically for the rolling metal shutters that would lock that evil away. Whoever had slid the shutters up last had pushed them so far, she had to jump to reach the string dangling from the end. Her fingers brushed against it — once, twice — before she finally caught hold and yanked down with all her might.

And, *wham!* Metal clanged against metal as the shutters hit the frame on the floor. She knelt and slid the bolt in, then froze, looking through the tiny slits between the shutters at the boots that appeared outside.

"Miss Boone, it is fruitless to attempt an escape," a man said as several others chanted behind him.

"Purity. Purity."

She fell back on her rear and scuttled backward. The door would hold them, but for how long? They could break through the windows. Bust through the back door.

Her body shook so hard, she could barely get to her feet.

"Purity. Purity..."

Even if she had plugged her ears with her fingers, the echo would still carry through. Who were these lunatics?

"Leave me alone!" she screamed, running her hands over her belly. *Leave my baby alone!*

The man at the door rattled the metal with his foot and laughed. "I'm afraid we can't, Miss Boone. I'm afraid you must die."

His voice was calm and steady, pure evil despite the easy tone.

"What did I do?" she screamed. "What did I do?"

She wanted to throw a chair at him. Pummel him with her fists. Find a big, heavy bat and swing it a few times. Why wouldn't these lunatics leave her alone?

"Humans are not permitted to mix with our kind. Not with wolves, not with bears. We must protect the purity of our bloodlines."

Wolves? Bears? Was he part of some secret society? Some kind of creepy military unit gone badly wrong?

She covered her stomach with her hands. The baby. They were after the baby. But why?

"Soren!" she screamed, even though he was too far to hear.

The man at the door gave a heavy sigh as the thugs who accompanied him spread out along the front windows, peering in under the letters that spelled *Blue Moon Saloon* backward from the inside looking out.

"He's part of the problem, my dear. Your whole twisted pack is the problem."

"You're the twisted one!" she screamed.

But screaming would get her nowhere, and she knew it.

Think, Sarah, think!

She spun around. She could run out the back, but who was to say there weren't more men out there? Even if there weren't, how long would she last? She wasn't exactly the fleet runner she used to be with the baby throwing her gait off.

The saloon was dim. A single light shone over the mirror of the bar. Her eyes hurried over the shelves, wondering what she could use to defend herself. A broken-off bottle? A stool?

The men outside moved slightly, and light glinted off the antique rifle hanging high above the bar. She stopped, staring at it as the sound of metal rolling against metal echoed in her mind.

Bullets. Soren kept silver bullets in the cash register.

She burst into action, running to the register. It opened with a ding and the rolling sound she was listening for. Soren had cleared out the money for the night, and she could see silver shining in the back. She scooped up a handful of bullets and threw them on the bar. One rolled off and plunked onto the rubber mat behind the counter as she scooped a second handful with shaking hands. Could she really shoot someone?

The open drawer of the cash register bumped her belly, reminding her of the baby, and she straightened quickly. Hell yes, she could.

The men outside shook the metal shutters by the door. Not a rattle of warning, as before, but powerful yanks that tested the strength of the bolt.

She pulled a stool over to the wall and climbed the rungs. Not quite as quickly as she'd once climbed trees, maybe, but faster than she bet any pregnant woman ever had. She got up on the back counter of the bar and reached for the rifle on tippy-toes. Her fingers slid off the polished walnut of the stock, and for one horrifying instant, she thought she'd fall.

Her arms flailed. Somehow, she ripped the rifle down and grabbed for a shelf at the same exact moment, then stood still, panting wildly. But only for an instant, because the men were milling around outside, preparing to attack. She could hear it in their voices, feel it in the charged air.

"Miss Boone..." that mocking voice called again.

It was only a small hop from the back section of the bar to the counter on which drinks were served, but it might as well have been the Grand Canyon as she eyed the bullets, lying so far away.

Go! Just go!

She half stepped, half jumped across the gap, knelt for the bullets, and started feeding them into the rifle's side gate.

Winchester, the stamp across the metal of the rifle's action declared. *1873.* Her dad would have paused to admire it, but she sure as hell didn't. She shoved in one bullet after another. Five? Six? She dropped one or two along the way, her hands were trembling that much. There were at least seven men outside, so she chambered another few rounds.

But her hands were shaking to high heaven, damn it, and her teeth were chattering, too. She cocked the gun with a resolute *click-click,* and that bolstered her a little. She had a .44 Winchester, damn it. She could scare these assholes away.

Assholes who had no weapons of any kind, it seemed, and yet they continued hammering at the door.

A booming crash sounded from the back, and she swung the rifle around. God, they were coming at her from both sides now. At least she was perched on the bar, high as a catwalk, though that was both a blessing and a curse. One false step and she'd fall.

She backed down the length of the bar, raising the rifle to shoulder level. Her finger found the trigger as she inched toward a wall in a balancing act that took half her concentration and all of her nerves.

A huge figure darted out from the back room and, *boom!* She fired.

The kick of the rifle nearly sent her tumbling off the counter. She gasped, and her target did, too.

"Jesus, Sarah!"

"Soren?" she screamed.

He popped up from where he'd dived to the floor. Unhurt, it seemed. He stared at her with wide eyes as her body started to melt down. God, she'd nearly shot Soren! What had she been thinking?

"Right idea." He nodded at the rifle, straightening to his full height. "Wrong target."

"Jesus, Soren!"

He went on as though she hadn't just made an awful mistake. "They set the fire as a diversion," he said, red with anger. Then he nodded at the rifle. "Take good aim."

"What?" She was thinking more along the lines of handing Soren the rifle and letting him do the shooting while she called the police and cowered in the back room.

Apparently, Soren had a different plan.

"Listen." His voice was urgent, his eyes blazing. "You need to aim carefully and take them out, one at a time."

She didn't want to take anyone out. She wanted to get the hell out. Both of them needed to get the hell out. Maybe by running out the back. . .

"Soren—"

His hands balled into fists. "This is it, Sarah. This is where we stop them. You and me."

He was serious. God, he was serious. And he was right. These lunatics had zigzagged across the country, following her. The only escape was to fight back.

She looked down at the rifle. It had gotten a shot off, so it worked. At least there was that.

One of the men outside the front raised his foot to kick in the window, and the rest backed up.

"Have you ever shot this thing?" she asked, swinging it toward the men.

"Once."

"Once?"

"It pulls a little high and to the right."

God, how could he be so calm? And what gun was he going to use?

"Do you have another weapon somewhere?" she yelped as the man outside kicked the glass. It rattled but held, to her surprise.

Soren's voice went all low and growly. "I'm about to let it out."

Let it out? Get it out? What did Soren mean?

"Look at me, Sarah," he said in that flat, calm voice.

How could she look at him when a lunatic was about to kick the window in?

"Look at me." His voice was so sure, so commanding, that she obeyed.

Soren took a deep breath. "Look at my eyes. Remember the color?"

She could have screamed in frustration. Of course, she remembered the color. No one else had eyes like that, except maybe his brother. The intense, honest blue, exactly the color of the sky back home.

"And remember this. Bears, good. Wolves, bad."

"Bears, what?"

"Bears, good. Wolves, bad. At least, these wolves are bad."

"What wolv—" she started to yell when the front window shattered.

Four men clambered in, and the others behind them continued that awful chant.

"Purity. Purity..."

Chapter Eighteen

Sarah swung the rifle around, cocked it quickly, and pulled the trigger.

Boom!

The first man through the windows ducked and rolled as the bullet buried itself in the wood above the busted windowpane.

"Aim for the heart," Soren told her in a strangely strangled voice.

She cursed. There were only so many bullets, and it sure looked like these men wouldn't back down from the sound alone.

Click-click. The spent cartridge sprang out, and she rammed a fresh one into place.

God, she'd really have to do it. She'd have to kill a man.

"Hurry, Soren!" she called, not daring to take her eyes off the intruders. What was taking him so long? Was the second weapon hidden somewhere hard to reach?

She took a deep breath, widened her stance, and took aim at a big man whose eyes locked on hers like the angel of death.

He wants to kill the baby, she reminded herself.

She squinted, pulled the trigger, then winced at the sound of the shot. She watched in shock as a dark shadow spread across the man's shirt. He stumbled back a step with a hand on his chest, strangely nonplussed.

"She thinks bullets can stop us," one of the others jeered.

They thought bullets *couldn't* stop them? How crazy were they?

The man she'd shot went from a sneer to gaping in disbelief, then crumpled to the floor.

"What? Jeff!" another one shouted and leaned over him.

They all hesitated for a moment, looking at the fallen man, and Sarah risked a glance to Soren on her left.

"Hurry, Sor—"

Her jaw fell open when she saw Soren hunch and groan.

Oh, God. Had he been shot, too?

His back curved as he fell to his hands and knees, half out of sight behind the bar. His shirt ripped right down the back and—

"Get them!" one of the men outside shouted.

She whipped back around, took aim at the nearest man, and pulled the trigger.

Ding! The bullet glanced off a copper light fixture just above him and to the right.

"Damn," she muttered, remembering what Soren had said about correcting to the left.

The dark-haired man ducked, then came up looking at her with rage in his eyes. His hair was shaggy, especially around the ears, like he'd gone far too long between trims and had chopped off the excess with a knife.

"You die," he hissed.

She was sure he'd come springing at her, but he just snarled. Really snarled like a dog and clawed at the air.

Soren growled, and she looked over again. Was he all right—

She froze in place at what she saw. Her heart thumped. Her blood slowed.

It was a trick of light. Or maybe she was hallucinating. Maybe she had finally lost her mind, because she'd just seen the last of Soren — the Soren she thought she knew every scar, every hair, every inch of — disappear under a thick, full pelt that seemed to sprout right out of his skin and swallow him up.

"Soren!" she cried.

He fell out of sight, and she prayed he'd stand up and wipe the illusion from her poor, bedraggled mind.

A snarl made her whip back around and raise the muzzle of the rifle. She pulled the trigger almost before focusing on her target, and this time, it was a direct hit. A black-haired wolf with shaggy ears grunted and fell flat.

She stared and felt sick. Where had the wolf come from? Where had the man gone? She didn't want to shoot a wolf. She'd been aiming at a man—

A rumbling, ferocious growl sounded from the end of the bar, and she looked back at Soren, then froze.

Not Soren. A bear. A massive grizzly with huge paws and golden ruff and—

It turned around to look at her with intense blue eyes, and she gasped.

Bears, good. The words echoed in her mind. *Wolves, bad.*

"Soren?" she peeped.

All hell broke loose as the bear jumped forward, setting off the fight. The saloon erupted into human shouts, canine barks, and ursine growls. Chairs and tables were shoved aside, and another shard of glass hanging from the front pane crashed to the ground.

"Get them!" the man in white yelled to the wolves.

Wolves, where a second before, there had been men.

Of course, she'd heard the stories spread by old-timer woodsmen back in Montana. Stories of humans who turned into wild animals — wolves, bears, lions. But she'd never, ever considered that they might be true.

She whipped the rifle to her shoulder and got off a shot just in time to ward off the nearest wolf, jumping toward her.

A distant corner of her mind told her they weren't regular wolves. They had matted, clumpy fur and burning red eyes. More like satanic dogs, if there were such a right thing.

Rogues, a voice that sounded just like Soren's echoed in her mind.

Whatever they were, they wanted her dead, so she had no choice but to shoot. Several attacked the bear while two others eyed her — cunning beasts who darted between tables, chairs, and even the pool table in the corner to stay out of her sights. One of the two ducked out of view while the other slunk behind the poker tables.

She cocked the rifle, aimed, and fired at his feet. And, *bam!* Wood splintered as a chair was blasted backward, toppling several others. The shot missed, though, and the wolf leaped right up onto the counter before she could cock the gun.

"No!" she cried, barely stepping clear.

The wolf snarled, then yelped as his claws scratched across the varnished surface the way a dog might slide across linoleum. Two of its four legs slid clear off the counter. Sarah struck out with a mighty kick and sent the beast toppling to the floor.

A roar that wasn't human or wolf but pure, angry bear thundered out. In the bar mirror, she saw it hurl a wolf right out the broken window, just under the spot where the shard with the word *Saloon* still hung precariously in the frame. She turned just in time to shoot the wolf springing at her from out of nowhere. It crashed into the side of the bar and fell out of sight.

Sarah spun back to the wolf that had fallen behind the bar and took a hasty shot as it darted into cover around the end.

"Damn it." Another miss.

For all the melee in the saloon, she could hear more voices chanting outside. "Purity. Purity."

God, how many more were there?

She spotted the gray-haired man in the white suit and raised the rifle. Hate pumped through her heart. The need for revenge. The need to stop the man who seemed to be over-seeing the attack from a safe distance — the man her heart told her had orchestrated the attack on her home.

He was right in her sights.

She aimed a little lower and to the left to correct for the rifle's error. She had him. She'd kill him. Now.

She squeezed the trigger.

Click.

One weak click of metal hitting metal, but nothing else. She'd spent all her ammunition.

"Shit!" she hissed.

"Get her!" the man in white yelled, seizing the moment.

Sarah jumped behind the counter and scrambled for the bullets she'd knocked to the floor. One...two...three... She threaded them into the gate, one by one. A fourth lay just out of reach, so she left it. She sprang up, banged the barrel of the rifle across the counter to keep it steady, and took aim at the man — a man this time, not a wolf — barreling at her from across the saloon with a knife in his hand.

His eyes went wide as she squeezed the trigger. The rifle kicked wildly as another shot hammered through the room.

Sarah stared, feeling sick as he fell to the floor.

There was no spreading pool of blood, though, no strangled cry. It was as if the bullet — the silver bullet — cut the lifeline of whatever mixture of man and beast that was.

Silver bullet... She shook her head, not quite able to admit what that might mean.

Concentrate!

She sighted along the rifle. The left side of the room was in chaos where the grizzly fought for... for...

Sarah stared. The grizzly wasn't fighting for his life. He was fighting for hers. Drawing the enemy away.

Soren was drawing them away.

Her mind superimposed the memory of Todd fighting for her in the same way at the fire back in Montana. Laying down his life just to give her a chance.

Wait, part of her mind coughed. *If Soren was a bear...*

She scanned the room for danger as her mind whirred away.

If Soren was a bear, could Todd have been a bear, too? They were cousins, those two.

A shadow moved between two tables, and she tracked it with the rifle, waiting for a shot.

Wait a minute, part of her mind protested. *How can anyone be a bear?*

But the rest of her brain followed the thoughts racing along like a runaway train.

If Todd was a bear, that meant...

Her heart just about leaped out of her chest as she made the connection. Soren — a bear. Todd — a bear. Her baby...

Jesus, could it be true?

A wolf moved into the open, and she pulled the trigger, then reloaded with a curse at her miss. One shot left.

ANNA LOWE

She shook every thought out of her mind and concentrated on the fight because that was all that mattered now. Everything centered around the bear, who raged and clawed and struck with fangs as long and thick as fingers. One wolf lay motionless on the floor, and another nursed a wounded foot. Three more were taking turns drawing the bear out to strike while the others leaped in, trying to get to its neck.

Her top lip lifted free of her teeth in a silent snarl of her own. She squinted down the barrel, waiting for a clear shot.

Soren, she told herself over and over. That was Soren, and she sure as hell wasn't going to clip him with a silver bullet tonight.

Two wolves closed on him at the same time, and she cried in alarm. The grizzly reared up on its hind legs and swiped a massive paw, scattering the wolves and sending one flying into a table that toppled and broke.

A cry slipped out of her throat as she registered the damage to the saloon. The saloon was Soren's new life, his livelihood. He and his brother and the others worked so hard to eke out an honest living here, and it was being destroyed.

Her finger squeezed the trigger before she even realized it, and the force of the shot sent a gray-black wolf toppling out the broken windowpane.

With a quick push-pull, she loaded the gun, but the movement didn't have the telltale resistance of the rest of her shots. The chamber was empty.

"Shit," she muttered, groping for another round in the cash register.

Ping!

Something whizzed past her ear. The bottle of Jim Beam behind her exploded into a thousand little bits.

The bear roared. She ducked. God, the attackers did have weapons, after all. And she'd put money on the fact that it was the gray-haired one. The one who kept safely out of the action. And she'd had him in her sights, damn it!

She scrambled on her hands and knees and picked up two more bullets from the edge of the rubber mat. The last two. And there were at least five wolves out there...

136

She peered cautiously out from the side of the counter, not over the top, where all she could see were the flanks of the bear and the quick feet of several wolves. Where was the man with the gun?

Putting her back to the inside wall of the serving counter, she slid upward, looking in the mirror as she went. There! The man in white stepped carefully through the jagged windowpane and entered the saloon with a pistol raised, looking for her.

Her heart slammed against her chest in an uneven, staccato beat. Should she risk leaping up and shooting him? Should she crawl out the side of the bar and get him by surprise? Should she—

The gray-haired man stopped and swung the pistol toward Soren, and she nearly shrieked. What if he was packing silver bullets, too?

She jumped, about to shoot, then caught herself when the grizzly sent another wolf flying. It dashed against the man in the white suit, who stumbled and fell from view.

"Shit," she murmured and quickly swung her head back to the bear. There'd been three wolves on him before, but now there were only two, and one moved just far enough right for her to—

She swung the rifle that way and shot. The kick of the weapon thumped into her shoulder, but she barely registered it. All that mattered was the sight of the wolf falling.

One shot left for two enemies: the wolf attacking Soren's back, and the leader of the gang, whom she could no longer see. She took a slow step out in front of the bar. Where was he? The bear-wolf brawl went on, not two yards away to her left, and she flattened herself against the side of the bar. She couldn't hide while Soren fought. She had to do her part, which meant finding the rogue leader and taking him out.

The left side of the bar was a blur of noise and motion, while the right was eerily still. Where was her enemy? She ducked, looking for his feet behind the pool table. Not there. By the windows? Not there. Over by the—

A chair came flying out of nowhere, and she ducked. Fast enough to protect her head, but not her shoulder, which took the bruising force of the blow.

She threw out her hands to stop her fall, and the rifle clattered to the floor, just out of reach.

A man snickered in the shadows. The bear roared.

She scrambled to her hands and knees, but she was too slow, too awkward. A shadow fell over her — a wolf, leaping in to attack. She'd been a fool, not paying attention to the wolves tossed aside by the bear. This one had been injured, but it was clearly not beaten.

She screamed as two-inch fangs spread wide, coming right for her.

A split second before she shut her eyes, a giant paw reached into view and batted the wolf aside, and another roar broke out. A huge mass stepped in front of her, glowering with rage. Even knowing it was Soren, it scared her stiff. He was so big. So furious. And Jesus, he was a bear.

His fur rippled and shone as he moved, and it would have been beautiful if she hadn't been so terrified. Two wolves closed in on him, one from each side, filling her ears with inhuman growls.

"Get him!" the man behind the wolves hissed.

Get him! her mind ordered her. *Get that evil man. Save Soren! Save the baby!*

A switch flipped inside her, and her blood went warm. Her muscles tensed, and a rush of power coursed through her. It was like the stories she'd heard of mothers performing superhuman feats — lifting cars off injured children or pulling them out of monstrous waves. Like all the power and energy she'd ever had at different points in her life rushed through time and space to fill her with a single overwhelming urge to act.

She dove for the rifle, and all the air whooshed out of her lungs when she landed on her ribs. But better her ribs than her stomach, so she bit back the pain.

Get on your feet and end this!

She rolled and lurched to her feet, shouldering the rifle in the same move. *Click-click.* She cocked the rifle, and everything morphed into slow motion. The bear rose to its hind legs, trying to shelter her. Its roar was muffled in her ears, as if tunnel vision pushed out sound, too. The man in white brought his pistol up, following the bear's motion, and his lips moved.

Purity. Purity.

A wolf growled somewhere far away.

Her mind superimposed cross hairs on the man's chest, and then she pulled down and to the left.

The bear all but blocked her shot, and she could have screamed at it. She knew what Soren was doing — laying his life down for her. But damn it, that was not going to happen. Not if she had her say.

She sidestepped for a clear shot, and every nerve in her body screamed as the man in white glanced her way.

Pull the trigger! Pull it now!

She squeezed.

The thump of her heart seemed louder than the crack of the rifle, and time moved so slowly, she swore she could see the bullet spiral through the air. She watched as it sped toward her enemy, as intent and determined as a living, breathing thing. As if it, too, needed this nightmare to end.

The gray-haired man's eyes widened as he registered the shot and brought his pistol around.

Too late. Sarah mouthed the words. He was too late. She squeezed her eyes shut an instant before the bullet hit.

The rest of her senses exploded back into real-time, though. She heard the man's dying grunt overlaid with the bear's bellow of triumph. The kick of the rifle punched her shoulder, throwing her against the bar. She slammed into it then slid to the floor. Claws scratched against the saloon tiles as the remaining wolf leaped at the bear, setting off the last skirmish of a losing battle. Then came a howl of pain, the patter of paws, and the quiet clink of broken glass as the last rogue fled through the front window of the saloon.

Then silence, except for the heavy beat of her heart.

Sarah sat on the floor, propped against the lower part of the bar. All the energy that had flooded into her body drained away as quickly as it had come. She couldn't think. Didn't really want to think, either. She just wanted to sit and breathe

ANNA LOWE

and shove reality away. Reality was too screwed up to fathom right now.

For a long minute, the saloon was blissfully silent, and she sat with closed eyes, blocking everything out.

Then something padded across the floor, and the air pressure around her changed as a big body moved into her space. A musky, animal scent filled her nostrils, along with a hint of oak, and she knew it was him. Soren.

He chuffed, asking her if she was okay.

She opened her eyes and nearly burst out cackling hysterically. No, she was not okay. She was ten inches away from a looming grizzly. All that fur filled her field of vision — overfilled it, almost, as if it wrapped behind her, too, and she nearly shrank away.

But when she caught sight of his eyes, she stopped short. Those eyes were a clear, honest blue, exactly the color of the sky back home. No one else had eyes like that.

"Soren," she whispered.

The bear's nose quivered, eight inches away.

He stretched forward ever so slowly, and when her hands flew up on instinct, he stopped, and his eyes dimmed with sorrow.

Did he think she might ward him off now? Did he think she was afraid?

Well, yes, she was afraid. Terrified, in fact. But not of him. She was terrified of what had just happened — and what the future might hold. But Soren? She loved him. Always had, always would.

She brought her hands up quickly and cupped his giant muzzle. She stroked the surprisingly silky fur with her thumbs and rubbed the broad cheeks with her fingers. His whiskers were bristly in the same way that the stubble on his chin would be, but his ears were soft and smooth.

His eyes warmed, pouring out gratitude and love, and he inched closer.

"Soren," she whispered again, telling herself it was real. Or maybe it was a dream, but that would be okay, too. As long as the nightmare was over and she had him.

The bear nuzzled her gently, up one side of her face and neck and down the other, and she laughed aloud. A content, rumbly sound came from his chest, and she hugged him closer, or as much of him as she could.

Soren was all right. Soren was a bear. A pretty damn ferocious one, but he was all cozy and cuddly now. Well, as cuddly as a bloody, injured bear could be.

She smiled and ruffled a clean patch of fur with her fingers. She could get used to the cozy part, for sure.

Her mind drifted with one scattered thought after another, and when she snapped herself back to reality, she was cuddled up with a man, not a bear.

She blinked at Soren's bare chest. His bare arms. His bare... bare everything, it seemed, though he hardly appeared to notice.

"Oh, God," she cried, seeing the tear across his shoulder and the bruise coloring his ribs. "Soren—"

"Shh." He touched her lips. "I'm fine."

"But—"

He shook his head and spoke quietly. "We heal pretty fast."

We? Part of her mind caught the hint, but another part shoved it away. There was only so much she could handle at once.

"So," she tried after a long, awkward minute passed. "Good bears, huh?"

He bit his lip. "I guess I have a lot to explain."

She nodded firmly. "Yes, you do. But not tonight. I've had enough for one night."

The minute she said it, something moved by the front windows, and Soren leaped to his feet. Her heart sank as more wolves jumped through the gaping hole. More attackers?

But instead of tensing, Soren relaxed, though his arm held her firmly behind him in a protective stance.

"It's okay," he murmured.

She wondered what could be okay about two wolves — no, worse — one wolf and one bear. A bear who reared up on its hind feet and... and... Slowly, gradually, the fur retreated

141

into skin, and there was Simon, looking around the wreckage of the saloon.

"Holy shit," he said.

The man was naked as the day he was born and not the least bit shy about it. Sarah dragged her eyes to the wolf at his side.

"Good wolf or bad wolf?" she whispered to Soren.

Simon chuckled. "I sometimes wonder myself."

The wolf growled, then shook its head vehemently.

"That's Jess," Soren said.

Sarah's eyes went wide. Jessica was a wolf? Simon was a bear?

Her mind spun, and she put a hand on Soren's arm, murmuring, "Holy shit."

Chapter Nineteen

Soren had a hell of a lot of explaining to do, and he knew it. But Sarah begged him not to try that night, so all he did was hang on to her and nuzzle her and show her it would be all right.

And it was. Somehow, it all was. It had to be.

Eventually, he would have to explain all about bears and wolves — and rogues and the Blue Bloods and everything else. But before he could even get her out of the wreckage of the saloon and up to her room to talk, several pickup trucks screeched to a stop in front of the saloon and a dozen men, women, and wolves rushed out.

Soren threw himself in front of Sarah, then exhaled when he saw who it was.

Sarah whispered from over his shoulder. "More wolves?"

"Good wolves," he nodded, keeping hold of her hand.

Ty Hawthorne came to a sudden stop in the doorway, taking in the shattered windows, upturned chairs, and lifeless rogues. "Whoa."

His mate, Lana, peered over his shoulder. "Whoa is right. Is everyone okay?"

Soren nodded wearily. "Everyone's okay."

He left out the *thank goodness* part, but damn, had it been a close call.

Ty Hawthorne's eyes burned into his after one more look around the saloon. A what-the-hell-happened-here stare that Soren returned cooly, squaring his shoulders at the same time. Ty might lead the most powerful wolf pack in the West, but this was Soren's turf. His clan, his victory.

The alpha wolf's eyes blazed, but gradually, the anger at being challenged ebbed away, and he nodded. A nod of respect, aimed Soren's way. Then Ty waved a hand over the doorway in a way that asked, *Mind if I come in?*

Soren savored the moment before responding. Ty's small gesture was a huge landmark; the equivalent of the alpha coming down the stairs of his own council house to receive Soren as an equal. Alpha to alpha.

He stood perfectly still, breathing the moment in.

When Sarah ran her hand down his arm, the glow building inside him grew warmer. Brighter. Prouder. Had he really done it? Had he finally earned his peace?

Soren glanced at Victor Whyte's lifeless body, then locked eyes with his brother.

Simon nodded with a weary grin. *Peace. Feels good, doesn't it?*

Soren held Sarah's hand in both of his. God, did it feel good.

"We got here as fast as we could," Lana said once Soren motioned the wolves of Twin Moon Ranch inside. So far, the fire around the block had kept outside attention away from the saloon, and he wanted to keep it that way. "A fire, broken windows, dead rogues? What happened?"

My amazing mate blew those assholes away, he wanted to say. But Sarah's hands were shaking. He needed to make this short and sweet and get her to a quieter, calmer place.

"The fire was a diversion." A diversion he'd nearly fallen for. If it hadn't been for Sarah's scream ripping through his mind, he might not have doubled back in time to help her. But damn, had she looked dangerous with that rifle.

Like a momma bear, all riled up. His bear nodded with pride.

"The tip-off we got about the Blue Bloods was a diversion, too." Ty scowled. "We took out the band of rogues heading to Yuma, but not the leaders."

If Soren had been closer to Victor Whyte's lifeless body, he might just have given it a vengeful kick.

"We took out the leaders," he said. *Sarah did,* he nearly added, remembering the bullet whistle past his ear to take out Whyte. But Sarah wasn't one to crow over a man's death, even if the man was a ruthless murderer. "We got Victor Whyte."

"Victor Whyte..." Sarah whispered.

He nodded. "The man who ordered the attacks in Montana. The one who had our families wiped out. We did it, Sarah. We stopped the Blue Bloods."

Ty Hawthorne's eyes focused on the Winchester laid across the bar, then on Sarah, and Soren could see him figure it out. The mighty alpha tipped his head at Soren, then at Sarah.

It should have been a moment of triumph, though all Soren felt was the exhaustion he saw mirrored in Sarah's eyes.

You got this? he asked Simon, getting ready to head upstairs.

Simon looked around the saloon. There were rogue bodies to get rid of, a sea of broken glass to clean up, a wolf pack to talk details with – and that was just for starters.

I got this, Simon nodded firmly. His eyes slid to Sarah, then back to Soren. *You got that?*

That, he knew, was the conversation he had to have with Sarah soon. Very soon.

He met her weary eyes, and she nodded at him. *Soon. But not tonight.*

With one last nod to Ty, Simon, and the others, Soren slid a hand across Sarah's shoulders and led her upstairs. To his bed, this time, where he'd barely gotten his arm around Sarah and the baby – His! Safe! Secure! – before falling into a fitful sleep.

∞∞∞∞

"Show me," Sarah demanded two days later. "Show me again."

She'd moved quickly from hollow-eyed shell-shock to quizzing him all about shifters, though it wasn't until the second night that she asked to see his bear.

"Show me," she repeated. So determined. So fierce. So brave.

Mate! his bear cheered. *My mate!*

He held his breath, made the slowest, quietest shift of his life, and prayed.

It's me, Sarah. He sent the thought into her mind as he shifted. *I love you. It'll be okay.*

Her eyes went wide and her lips pursed as she studied him, and he'd never felt more self-conscious in his life. He kept his fangs carefully tucked behind his lips and his claws as deeply hidden as he could. Tried to make his bear body as small as possible, though that was a losing battle.

Sarah reached out one shaky hand, took a deep breath, and started petting his bear body. Tentatively at first then more boldly, until she ended with both hands around his muzzle and her eyes firmly locked on his.

I love you, Sarah. It's me.

And just when he thought that she'd turn her back and shun him forever, she hugged him. An all-out, human-to-bear hug like he'd never tried before. And God, he'd never felt so good. Her warm breath ruffled his fur, her hands smoothed the coarse pelt of his back, and she murmured his name over and over.

"God, Soren. Soren..." She seemed to want to say more, but all she got out was his name, and that was enough.

His bear didn't dare move. Barely dared to breathe, but inside, he was doing a happy dance.

She loves me! Me!

So his being a bear – thank every star in heaven – seemed to be okay with her.

Then there was the part about the baby, and that was harder. Sarah went awfully quiet when he shifted back to human form and explained that even half shifter blood was enough to make the baby a werebear, and that it would eventually be able to shift, too.

Sarah kept her eyes on the floor while he did his best to explain that a clan was a clan and all the advantages that brought. The best kind of tight-knit family in the world, forever. No matter how he tried to explain, though, Sarah rested her hands on her stomach, looking pensive and unsure.

But then Janna — who he could just about kiss sometimes — brought Sarah a little teddy bear and a ridiculously furry toy wolf. Janna and Jessica kicked him out of the room and talked to Sarah for hours. About girl stuff, he supposed, though he never figured there'd be so much to cover. The room was quiet for a while, then peals of laughter bounced through the walls, interspersed with naughty giggles.

Simon walked by with a faraway look that said his mind was communicating with his mate, and he moaned. "Jesus, I thought only guys talked about that stuff." Simon rapped sharply on the door. "Jess! No need to share every detail, right?"

"Every detail of what?" Soren asked.

Simon rolled his eyes. "They're telling Sarah about mating bites." He thumped Soren on the chest. "I'm out of here."

Cole followed him with an apologetic look, wincing at whatever thought Janna had shot into his mind. "Do you have to share everything, honey?"

Soren stared at the door for a while, caught somewhere between arousal and despair. Shifter pairs shared mating bites to seal their bond, and it was said to be an incredible high, especially when coupled with the peak of sex. He'd dreamed of biting Sarah in a thousand dusky fantasies. But shifters grew up with those stories and knew there was no danger, only a rush. How would Sarah feel about the idea?

He paced the hallway like a goddamn expectant father outside a delivery room while the women chatted for hours. When the door finally opened, he jumped away and stood in guilty silence.

"Well, well. What do we have here?" Janna scolded.

Jessica burst into giggles. "How long have you been waiting around here, bear?"

He craned his neck and saw Sarah behind them, hiding a smile as the other two cackled away. At him. Him, the alpha of this clan!

The crazy thing was, he laughed too. Out of sheer relief, because it didn't look like Sarah was packing her bags or edging out the door.

Then he coughed and glared out of the principle of the thing to shoo the two she-wolves away. He stepped into the room, shut the door, and walked to Sarah, who was sitting on the bed with the stuffed animals. He sat down beside her, leaving her a little space.

"Um... You okay with all this bear stuff?" he tried after a pause.

She smiled and pulled him closer. "You know I have a thing for bears."

And damned if her voice wasn't husky, her eyes bright.

As much as he gulped, the lump sitting in his throat refused to go down.

"I wanted to tell you so many times," he said. "I hated keeping it from you. But... but... " He shook his head at all those years full of *buts*, ashamed of each and every one.

Sarah pulled him closer, and they sat there, forehead to forehead, letting another minute tick quietly by.

"I'm good with bears." Sarah nodded. "If you're good with... " Her hand slipped to her stomach, and she drew away from him.

He pulled her right back. It was time he tore down the brick wall standing between them, once and for all.

"How could I not be good with something that's part of you?"

She squeezed her lips together, and he could see the doubt in her mind, hear the unspoken words. *But this baby isn't yours.*

He took a deep breath and slowly, carefully, put his hand on her belly. "Todd would have taken care of my child like it was his own. I'll take care of his the same way."

When Sarah glanced up at him looking sadder than ever, he shook his head firmly and went on. "Not because I have to. Because I want to. Because it's yours. Because this baby is clan."

She looked so desperately hopeful, yet still so scared, so he plunged on.

"Because the baby is my... my... " He searched for the word.

148

Mine? his bear suggested.

He pictured Sarah standing on the bar with the shotgun, surrounded by rogues, and had to fight away a flood of rage and fear that threatened to wash over him all over again. He'd fought for the baby as much as he fought for Sarah. He couldn't bear the thought of losing either of them.

"Mine," he said firmly. "The baby is mine."

Sarah's fingers tightened over his.

"I mean, I want the baby to be mine. It feels like mine." God, was he even getting it all out right? "I'll make it mine, if you'll let me. I mean... "

And thank God Sarah put a finger over his lips then, because he was stuck, damn it. Again.

"Soren."

He looked at her. Christ, now he was the desperately hopeful one.

She nodded. "I want the baby to be yours."

"You do?" His heart thumped a little faster as his bear started bouncing inside.

Mine!

Another nod. "Just like I want to be yours. Like I want you to be mine."

"I already am yours." She was his one, his only. Always had been, always would be.

She drew a finger down his cheek and smiled. Almost a little sultry, that grin. And just like that, his inner thermometer flipped right over to hot.

"I mean, all the way yours, my love."

He blinked at her. "All the way? As in... "

She rounded her hands over his shoulders and pulled him close.

"All the way," she whispered in his ear.

The scent of her arousal filled his nose. Filled the whole room, and his swooped in right on its heels. He was hard already. Hungry. So, so ready to claim his mate.

"All the way, as in... " he murmured, pushing her back to the mattress. God, seeing her look up at him that way...

149

"As in, a mating bite," she said at last, nibbling his ear. "Jess and Janna said it was pretty amazing."

He snorted. "Only pretty amazing?"

She laughed, and the last bit of tension slipped off his shoulders.

"I'll show you amazing," he said, claiming her lips with his.

Then it was his turn to stay locked up in that room with Sarah for hours, and it wasn't to talk, except maybe with actions and deeds. Like long, lingering kisses to her belly and her breasts. Like peeling off her clothes, one layer at a time, and nuzzling her all over, marking her as his.

"God, you're beautiful," he murmured in her ear. Her eyes were closed, her head tipped back, and when his lips closed over her nipple—

"Oh!" she cried, and her whole body rose.

Her hands flitted all over him, not quite focused on one thing. Which only wound him up tighter, those fleeting little touches to his shoulders, his rear, his chest. When she closed her fist around his hard, aching cock, he groaned.

Make her ours! his bear roared inside.

God, he was so, so close to coming. So, so close to biting. To making her his forever. But he wasn't going to rush this even if it killed him.

The hand that had been kneading her breast slid over her belly and past her mound. Familiar ground, but still, it felt like their first time.

My beautiful, beautiful mate, his bear chanted as he ran a finger through her folds.

"Soren," she moaned, writhing under him.

God, she was amazing. She'd faced down the Blue Bloods like a warrior, but now she was all woman again.

All mine. Mine!

His cock ached when he touched her inside, impatient to slide into that tight, hot sheath.

Take her! Make her mine!

"Soren," she panted, throwing her head back. He looked up at all that white, unblemished skin, and his heart rate jumped.

Bite her. Take her. Make her mine.

How he'd resisted the urge so many times in the past, he didn't know. His canines extended, and he couldn't hold them back. Didn't want to hold them back.

"Do it," she cried. "Bite me. Make me yours."

He ducked his head against her chest and panted there for a second or two. "Mating is forever, Sarah. And it would make you a bear, too," he managed to rasp out between heavy breaths. Did she understand that? Was she sure?

"I always wanted forever," Sarah said. "I always wanted you."

Every muscle in his body screamed for him to bite. This was the moment. No more waiting. No more hoping. No more wishing.

He climbed back up her body and all but smothered her in a kiss, and she arched against him, begging for more.

"Sarah," he growled, assuring himself this was real and not another dream.

So, so real, his bear howled. And better than any goddamn dream.

"Soren," she groaned, pushing her hips against his.

Make her ours now!

He kissed her throat a dozen times as he turned her as gently as his half-crazed bear could be convinced to do and pulled her onto all fours. When she arched her back and raised her head, her hair cascaded to one side, exposing her neck.

There, his bear cried, honing in on the smooth flesh. *Right there.*

He kneeled behind her, running his hands over her rear. Sliding into place.

"Soren," she mumbled.

He plunged in, and her voice rose to a cry of delight.

"God, yes. Yes. . . "

Her hips jammed against his, and she might as well have yelled, *Deeper! Faster!*

Mate! My mate!

He thrust in and out until her cries steadied out and they both fell into a rhythm, rocking at exactly the same time.

"Yes. . . "

He leaned forward and let his teeth scrape her neck.

"Bite me," she breathed.

He pushed her hair aside and licked her skin, almost exploding at the barrage of sensations. The tight squeeze of her inner muscles against his cock. The hot slide as he thrust in and out. The soft weight of her breast in his hand, and the scent of her, most intense right there at her neck.

She called to him with her body, her voice, and her mind. *Take me, my love.*

He pulled his lips back, settled his mouth over her neck, and let his teeth break the skin. As slowly and carefully as he could while still pounding into her from behind, because he couldn't stop that any more than he could stop breathing or reveling in the pleasure-pain.

There was no cry of horror, no gushing blood. Nothing but Sarah's deep moan of pleasure and a steady pulse under his teeth. Her life force, calling to him.

Destiny, his bear said. *Destiny wants this.*

He couldn't doubt it, because her flesh parted as if it had been waiting for his bite for all these years. Years!

He bit deeper, keeping his lips sealed over her skin.

His hips pumped harder and harder, and every muscle in him tensed as he exploded inside her.

Mate! My mate!

It was a high like he'd never experienced or even imagined. A connection that went beyond the points of his teeth and his pulsing cock to reach deep, deep into his soul.

"Sarah." He held her tight against his body as she shuddered and cried.

Release. Sweet, sweet release. The invisible weight that had been pressing down on his soul for so long he'd stopped noticing it lifted and fluttered away like an oversated bird of prey. Everything fluttered away. The room, the light, and the sounds of the street below. Everything but the feel of Sarah connected to him.

She murmured his name again and again, then shook with a second aftershock. He held on to the mating bite all through

152

it and the next, then slowly, slowly released her when she went limp under him.

They collapsed on their sides, squeezed together as tightly as exhausted limbs allowed, and he kissed her neck a dozen times as she all but purred under his touch.

"So, so good," she mumbled in a daze.

So, so mine, he wanted to say.

So say it, his bear prodded him. *She is.*

He closed his eyes and relished that feeling, that truth. It was in the tingle on his skin, and the glow around their bodies. Finally — finally! — Sarah was his. He was hers. Forever.

He smoothed a hand over her cheek and curled closer.

"Mine," he whispered. "My beautiful mate."

When she sighed and turned to peek at him over her shoulder, he just about melted at the love in her eyes.

"What are you looking at?" she murmured. Her eyes were glowing, her pulse skipping under his hand.

"You," he whispered. "You."

Epilogue

Four months later...

Sarah yawned and cracked an eye open. What was that humming sound?

She let her eyes roam sleepily, bringing the room into focus. The pale pink light of dawn filtered through the curtains hung over the arched windows, lighting up the bookshelves along one wall. Real bookshelves, because they'd finally turned the bare walls of her room into a homey space. Soren's room had become their own private living room, and the third room in their corner of the meandering apartment over the saloon was the nursery, though they hadn't gotten around to moving the crib yet. It was still in their bedroom, near the crescent moon night-light glowing faintly in a corner of the room. That was the corner where the hum came from, along with the faint creak of a rocking chair.

A little gurgle sounded, and the hum broke off.

"Shh," Soren whispered to the bundle snuggled close to his chest. "Mommy's sleeping."

She hid her smile and watched as he nuzzled the baby with his nose. Soren barely fit into the chair, and the baby seemed too tiny for his massive hands, yet he looked so comfortable, so at home. So at peace.

"We gotta let Mommy sleep. Daddy's got you," he murmured and started humming again.

The deep, quiet bass carried through the room, and she nearly hummed back. Soren's hum didn't just soothe the baby — it soothed her, too. She went warm all over, and sleepy, too.

155

It was Monday, thank goodness, a day off for both the saloon and the café. A slow day for everyone in her little pack.

Pack, clan; whatever. Jess and Janna liked to call their budding little group a pack, while Simon and Soren insisted on calling it a clan. Cole was carefully neutral about it all, using both terms interchangeably. And Sarah — well, she just called it home. A home free from fear and anxiety now that the Blue Bloods were gone. Really gone. It was a home full of boundless love for the baby — not just her love, but Soren's, too. Soren's and everyone's, in fact. If she didn't watch it, the baby would grow up spoiled rotten.

"My little teddy bear," Jess would call him when she and Janna argued over who got to babysit when.

"My little teddy," Janna would shoot back.

"My little Teddy," Soren would growl, staking his claim. Then he'd hold the baby close and whisper to him. "My little Teddy."

A whisper. A promise. A bright future. Sarah sighed, just thinking about it.

Soren had been all for naming the baby Todd, but she had insisted on taking one step away from that name to Ted, who went by Teddy for now. The important thing, she figured, was to be honest with the child about who he was and how he came to be, not to burden him with the past.

But all that explaining would come later, as the baby grew up. Now, all that mattered was making him feel loved. That, and getting sleep, because the little guy was a champion milk guzzler, and he'd been up twice in the night already. Just trying to keep up with him wore her out.

Soren caught her yawning and shot her a smile.

Morning, he said, sending the words right into her mind.

That was one of the many advantages of being a shifter — she and Soren could communicate without disturbing the baby. And that was just for starters. She'd only shifted into bear form a few times so far, and as awkward as she felt coordinating four feet, Soren looked at her like she was the most beautiful creature that had ever been placed on the earth.

The way he was looking at her now, even though her hair was a tangled mess and her face wrinkled with pillow lines.

Morning, she called back. Her heart swelled in her chest, just from looking at him. Her man. Her baby. Her family, safe and secure.

Mine, mine, mine, said the voice she'd come to recognize as her inner bear's. It was exactly like her voice, just an octave deeper, and nowhere near as jarring as it had been at first. The bear was part of her now. In a way, it always had been.

Every person has an animal inside, Soren had explained to her, early on. *Being a shifter just brings it out.*

Which made sense. On that awful night of the Blue Blood attack, she'd called forth an inner fury and courage she didn't even know she possessed.

Of course, thinking like a bear and actually turning into one were two very different things, and she'd nearly panicked the first time she tried shifting forms. Did she really want to feel her teeth rip through her gums or see her hands turn into paws? On the other hand, part of her was eager to shift, too — the animal part, she supposed. But it was too risky to shift until after the baby was born, so she'd had an excuse to put off trying for a while.

"Ready?" Soren had asked her, the first time he'd taken her up into the national forest to shift after the baby was born.

Ready, her bear had growled, and she'd nearly jumped out of her skin, hearing its voice boom through her mind. *So, so ready.*

Jessica and Janna had been thrilled to babysit for a few hours, so she was out of excuses, and the inner itch had grown to a point that was impossible to ignore. So she took a deep breath and nodded.

"Tell me what to do."

"Um..." Soren seemed stuck on that for a while. As a born shifter, he'd never had to think about shifting. "Think furry thoughts?"

Which got her absolutely nowhere, of course. But then Soren flooded her mind with a dozen images. Scents and sounds, too, like the sweet nectar of wildflowers, the delicious

157

crackle honeycomb made when you bit it into chunks. The blissful sensation of grass tickling her belly when she was bent over on all fours, and—

Holy crap, she'd blurted, seconds later. *I'm a bear.*

She really was a bear. She'd done it.

World's most beautiful bear, Soren said, looking about as proud as he did when he held the baby.

He made her shift back and forth between human and bear forms. With his coaching, shifting had been much easier than she expected. Thrilling, even, to be that in tune with nature and to possess such power. They'd taken off on a long stroll through the mountains, side by side, and she felt drunk on the impressions flooding her keen bear senses.

"I did it! Did you see that? I did it!" she'd cried out when they shifted back at the end of the night.

Soren had grinned from ear to ear, watching her, then held her tight. "I knew you could." The man had such limitless faith in her, it was scary.

But he was right. Shifting had seemed as scary as motherhood had, but she'd slipped right into that role, too. She knew just how to hold the baby, how to coo to him, when to hold him close, and when to lay him down.

Everything was falling into place. Her, Soren, and the baby had become a content little unit of three within a warm and accepting clan of seven.

"Not the biggest clan in history," Soren had once said, shaking his head.

"Maybe not the biggest, but the best," Janna had replied.

"And we're going places. Right, sweetie?" Jessica had agreed, nuzzling the baby as if he were her own.

They were going places. Everyone had pulled together to patch up the saloon, and business was booming there and at the café. Thanks to her enhanced healing abilities — another plus of having turned shifter — she'd bounced right back from the trying experience of childbirth and got back to work within a few weeks. Soren cared for the baby in the mornings, and she took over in the afternoons. It might have been grueling, but it worked well since they could check in with each other throughout the day.

"Finally, an advantage to running your own business," Soren had said, more in pride than complaint.

Still, Mondays were the best. Sarah stretched, reveling in the feel of the soft cotton sheet on her bare skin. Bare all over, because there wasn't much point in wearing PJs only to take them off the minute her mate got frisky — or when she was the one turning up the heat. Another side effect of being a bear, she supposed — not only had she recovered from childbirth quickly, her libido came roaring back with a vengeance not long after they'd settled in with their newborn.

Mmm, her inner bear rumbled, already thinking of all the fun she could have with her mate once he came back to bed. She'd start by nuzzling him — and God, was Soren a champion nuzzler — then move on from there.

A beautiful morning, she said to her mate.

When Soren nodded quietly, his cheeks glowed with more than just the golden dawn light. He didn't say much — Soren never did — but he held up the baby's hands and feet, going over each tiny digit as if it was a miracle of its own. He murmured something too low to hear and kissed the top of the baby's head, then laid him in the masterpiece of a crib he'd spent hours making in the woodshop. Soren had fussed over every detail of it, insisting the baby deserved the best. He stood there for a long time, adjusting the blanket, the pillow, and a half-dozen unnecessary things. Then he climbed back in the bed and curled around her.

"Good morning," he rumbled, right in her ear.

She rolled and hooked her leg around his, grinning up at him. "Yes, it is, my love. Yes, it is."

Sneak Peek: Salvation

One hero, assumed dead. One woman who refuses to give up. One destiny.

Anna Boone won't give up the search for her cousin, Sarah, who everyone assumes dead. And she refuses to give up on the wounded bear found next to the ashes of her cousin's house. There's something deep in his eyes and in his soul she just can't resist. Something special. Something... human, almost. When her search for the truth leads her to the Blue Moon Saloon, Anna finds more than she ever bargained for — and unwittingly leads a deadly foe to those she loves most.

Get your tissues ready and order your copy of SALVATION today! Available as ebook, paperback, and audiobook!

Books by Anna Lowe

Blue Moon Saloon

Perfection (a short story prequel)

Damnation (Book 1)

Temptation (Book 2)

Redemption (Book 3)

Salvation (Book 4)

Deception (Book 5)

Celebration (a holiday treat)

Aloha Shifters - Jewels of the Heart

Lure of the Dragon (Book 1)

Lure of the Wolf (Book 2)

Lure of the Bear (Book 3)

Lure of the Tiger (Book 4)

Love of the Dragon (Book 5)

Lure of the Fox (Book 6)

Aloha Shifters - Pearls of Desire

Rebel Dragon (Book 1)

Rebel Bear (Book 2)

Rebel Lion (Book 3)

Rebel Wolf (Book 4)

Rebel Heart (A prequel to Book 5)

Rebel Alpha (Book 5)

Fire Maidens - Billionaires & Bodyguards

Fire Maidens: Paris (Book 1)

Fire Maidens: London (Book 2)

Fire Maidens: Rome (Book 3)

Fire Maidens: Portugal (Book 4)

Fire Maidens: Ireland (Book 5)

The Wolves of Twin Moon Ranch

Desert Hunt (the Prequel)

Desert Moon (Book 1)

Desert Blood (Book 2)

Desert Fate (Book 3)

Desert Heart (Book 4)

Desert Rose (Book 5)

Desert Roots (Book 6)

Desert Yule (a short story)

Desert Wolf: Complete Collection (Four short stories)

Sasquatch Surprise (a Twin Moon spin-off story)

Shifters in Vegas

Paranormal romance with a zany twist

Gambling on Trouble

Gambling on Her Dragon

Gambling on Her Bear

Serendipity Adventure Romance

Off the Charts

Uncharted

Entangled

Windswept

Adrift

Travel Romance

Veiled Fantasies

Island Fantasies

visit www.annalowebooks.com

About the Author

USA Today and Amazon bestselling author Anna Lowe loves putting the "hero" back into heroine and letting location ignite a passionate romance. She likes a heroine who is independent, intelligent, and imperfect – a woman who is doing just fine on her own. But give the heroine a good man – not to mention a chance to overcome her own inhibitions – and she'll never turn down the chance for adventure, nor shy away from danger.

Anna loves dogs, sports, and travel – and letting those inspire her fiction. On any given weekend, you might find her hiking in the mountains or hunched over her laptop, working on her latest story. Either way, the day will end with a chunk of dark chocolate and a good read.

Visit *AnnaLoweBooks.com*

Printed in Great Britain
by Amazon

58565038R00109